SHE WHO MUST BE OBEYED

FEMME DOMINANT
LESBIAN EROTICA

SHE WHO MUST BE OBEYED.

FEMME DOMINANT LESBIAN EROTICA

edited by D. L. King

LETHE PRESS
MAPLE SHADE, NEW JERSEY

Published in 2014 by LETHE PRESS, INC.
118 Heritage Avenue, Maple Shade, NJ 08052 USA
lethepressbooks.com / lethepress@aol.com

ISBN: 978-1-59021-249-3 / 1-59021-249-5

"Tears from Heaven" by JEAN ROBERTA was previously published under the title "Mourning Becomes Athena" in *Philogyny* (2010), copyright © 2012 JEAN ROBERTA / "Uncharted Territory" by EVAN MORA was previously published in *Under Her Thumb: Erotic Stories of Female Domination* (2013), copyright © 2013 EVAN MORA. All other stories are original to this volume.

INTERIOR DESIGN: Matt Cresswell
COVER DESIGN: Niki Smith.

CONTENTS

INTRODUCTION
D. L. King

Ask a lot of butches and they'll tell you that the premise of this book is all wrong. In fact, they may be totally squicked by it. But I submit to you that perhaps you are asking the wrong butches. Okay, no *perhaps* about it. Make no mistake, there are plenty of women who place their femmes on a pedestal, who look to them for guidance and want nothing more than a take-charge lady in the bedroom.

The dominant femme has long been an archetype in life, as well as in literature. Butches, bois, women and girls look to her as the guiding force in life and love and, of course, hot, down and dirty, back-up-against-the-wall sex. And dominant women know, perhaps innately, that bois need a firm, guiding hand. The same holds true for butches of all stripes as well as girls and other women. It's a universal truth that the dominant femme knows just where she fits and all others will flock to the aura of power surrounding her.

You know, as do I, the time has come for a book like this. You know how difficult it is to find yourself in literature. Sure, you can reverse roles: put a flowery dress on the butch wielding the whip and tighty whities, showing the clear outline of a well-packed package on the femme kneeling at his feet—but it's not the same, is it? Not the same as having your own story with the roles correctly portrayed as you live them.

And yes, you thought right when you thought BDSM. After all, when I say *femme dominant*, that's what I'm talking about. However, there's a real mix here. These stories are about predilections for mild spankings to intense SM and everything in between. It's a very eclectic mix, perhaps my most eclectic anthology to date.

In Valerie Alexander's story, "Noir," our hero finds herself the entertainment at a very *A List* Hollywood party—the entertainment for one very particular guest.

Mary Tintagel's story is about skydiving. But this is very unusual skydiving. All I can tell you is that it's exciting, thrilling and not a little cold. But you'll have to find out for yourself.

There are stories about rodeo riders and horse trainers; ballerinas and bosses. Karen Taylor sets the scene with a "Garden Party" thrown by a femme for her femme friends and their partners and playthings. She charges her two butches with the task of making sure everything is perfect for her guests. They are both very different bois with very different talents.

How about a roaring 20's murder mystery fundraiser, complete with a gorgeous blonde dame sporting three bodyguards and a rough-around-the-edges young boi who takes quite a shine to her. Styx St. John's story incorporates everything from retro drinks, great costumes, candy cigarettes and cigars, so as not to break any clean air ordinances to hot sex.

Jean Roberta's Athena Chalkdust metes out some tough academic discipline in "Tears from Heaven" and Evan Mora explores "Uncharted Territory" with her story about first-time anal sex. These are just a few of the authors whose masterful stories will get your blood racing. There are stories by a lot of your favorite writers here but there are also quite a few folks you may never have read before. In fact, I'm happy to tell you that I am the first to publish one of these authors, but I'm sure I won't be the last.

So cuddle up with your sweet baby and read some bedtime stories, just be ready to lose your place at some point.

D. L. King
New York City

b

NOIR

Valerie Alexander

SHE'S A REAL FILM GODDESS STANDING BEHIND THE BAR. Waving dark hair, deep green eyes, pillowy lips. All wrapped up in strapless black satin like a dangerous gift. In my mind she's undressing me like a goddess should, lifting up my man's undershirt to touch my nipples and then taking down my jeans. Except it's a bit rough and unsensual because of her black opera gloves. I yearn for her bare fingertips on my clit—but I haven't yet earned that privilege.

"Did you want a drink, miss?"

I give the server a cold stare, both for interrupting my reverie and for calling me miss. "Yeah, a Dr. Pepper. And I'll have the club sandwich."

Unbelievable to think I came in here for someone else. I met Heather last weekend, a cute femme in a Wonder Woman tank top and pink pigtails who bought me a shot. She screamed over the music about the restaurant she worked in, a café where all the waitresses dressed up like silver screen stars. So I promised to come see her. I even tried to request her section tonight but instead the hostess put me with a waitress dressed as Jayne Mansfield. It doesn't matter now. As soon as I looked behind the bar at Ava Gardner in her black strapless gown, all overflowing cleavage and long dark hair, I was a goner.

"Dijon on your sandwich?"

"No." I wish she would leave and bring me my drink, so I can slam it down and go to the bar for a refill.

The Jayne Mansfield server leaves and I try to catch Ava's eye.

Her beautiful face is staring out the window, ignoring the tables where straight men—or smitten young butches like me—are gaping at her. What incredible bone structure.

1

I head up to the bar and her green eyes meet mine. "Your server will take your drink order," she says flatly.

"I—she did already." My mind fails me utterly. There's nothing else to say. But I can't just turn around and go back to my table with my tail between my legs.

Ava stares at me. Nothing, not a smile or an eyebrow flicker greets me. And to my humiliation, her disdainful stare makes my heart beat faster and my nipples go stiff.

"You did come!"

It's Heather from last weekend—or rather, Lana Turner, in a push-up bra and platinum wig.

Dammit, I was hoping she hadn't noticed me. "I requested you, but Jayne Mansfield is my server." Fifteen minutes ago I would have been totally thrilled to bang this girl. Now she's just a hindrance to true love.

But Ava actually has a facial expression now—she's glancing from Heather to me with a small, amused smile. She's a reader of situations, Ava is.

"That dumbass hostess has been mixing us up all night! Here, I'll change tables with Leslie."

"Don't bother." It sounds so graceless. Heather looks hurt. "I mean, I don't want to cause any trouble."

"It's not any trouble," she beams and rushes off.

Was she so eager and shrill in the bar last weekend? I try to think of a clever remark for Ava. But she's giving me a smile of amused contempt.

"It's not nice to be fickle," she says.

"Who's fickle? I haven't done anything," I say defensively.

"You didn't come in here to meet up with Heather, then change your mind when you got a look at the *much hotter* bartender?"

She leans over the bar as she says that last part, cradling her luscious tits and smiling deep into my eyes.

My throat goes dry. Confident women have always been my weakness. And when she runs one scarlet fingernail across my bottom lip, I feel physically faint; I'm ready to sign over my every possession to her.

"I'm your slave," I say.

This is actually a real line I often give to girls in bars, because femmes love nothing like they love being admired. But usually I deliver it with a certain flirtatious swagger. Tonight it just sounds helpless. "You're the most perfect woman I've ever seen." I try again, though it doesn't sound any better.

She smiles for real now, a white, predatory grin.

"And what are you willing to do for the most perfect woman you've ever seen?" she says, still tracing my mouth.

"Anything." It's true, even if I've gone from helpless to desperate.

Her green eyes drop to my cotton undershirt. My impressive weight-trained biceps, my less impressive skinny hips. Then lift to meet my gaze again.

"Midnight, the alley out back. Don't be late."

◯◯◯

WHEN I COME BACK AT 11:52 PM, THE CAFÉ IS DARK AND THE ALLEY IS EMPTY. There's a few cars parked out back, but everyone seems to have gone home. Fog is rolling through L.A., obscuring the grime of the alley, the hulking dumpster, the boarded-up windows of the adjoining building.

She walks out still in the black strapless gown and opera gloves.

She gives me that head to toe assessment again and then gives my shoulder a push downward.

"Get on your knees."

So it's going to be like that. Her earlier femme fatale act wasn't just flirting. I pause, because even though I fantasize ruthlessly about being commanded and controlled by an aggressive femme, there's a certain mercilessness in those green eyes. Suddenly I feel certain that this might end in a screaming orgasm or a plea for mercy, but it probably won't end with a cuddle before brunch.

I get on my knees, the asphalt cold and damp through my jeans.

She pulls up her dress and shows me pale, shapely long legs and then the smooth seashell of her pussy. Of course she's waxed bare. She's the most flawlessly groomed woman I've ever seen.

She smiles down at me. "Get to work—and if you do a good job, there's a reward in it for you."

It goes unsaid that there might be a punishment if I do a bad job. She really is a piece of work, one of those beautiful women who've been so spoiled by lifelong adoration that they're incapable of viewing less aesthetically blessed mortals as equals. And who is she to treat me like a servant? I might not have her killer bone structure, but I do perfectly fine with the girls of Los Angeles. Plenty of them have told me my dashing butch charms are hard to come by in these parts. Certainly I've never had to try hard to get laid. Numerous ex-girlfriends, my college roommate's mother, the long-legged volleyball player who gave me her number last week—I am plenty in demand myself and I want Ava to know it.

But I can't deny that the fog and the silence and her imperious stare are sending a rush through my blood. Without another word, I sweep my tongue over her entire pussy. She tastes surprisingly sweet given her bitchy attitude. Her clit is teeny when I pop it out of its hood and her pussy, when I slide inside, closes around my fingers like tight velvet. And she's drenched, the slick honey on my fingers belying the aloof coolness of her voice. She wants me like I want her, maybe not quite as adoringly, but the creamy heat gracing my tongue doesn't lie. Maybe she just likes putting young blond butches on their knees in dark alleys, maybe she likes dominating anyone, but at this moment, her body is surrendering to my mastery. Which melts my nervous desire to impress her into confidence and I lick and fuck her that much harder, buried in her animal heat and her smell.

She grips my short blond hair, what she can get of it. And in the darkness of her thighs, I smile, because I can feel her trembling and gasping as that high-femme disdain evaporates beneath my expertise. Her body tenses for three moments, four, and then she cries out and doubles over, her pussy contracting around my fingers in a gush.

After licking her clean, I sink back on my heels with a smile. "About that reward."

And then an intense light bathes both of us, making me fall back and shield my eyes. I get to my feet, wiping my mouth and staring at the parked black Lexus that just turned its headlights on us. Apparently we've had an audience the entire time.

The Lexus pulls up between us. "Get in," Ava says, sliding into the backseat. I pause, knowing now she is most definitely shady, a villainess in black satin with an agenda that can't be benevolent. I don't even know her real name. But my clit is still twinging with desire and my tongue is sweet with her taste, so I get in the car.

CRWD

THE LEXUS TRAVELS UP INTO THE CANYON, THE HEADLIGHTS MOVING OVER scrub and the occasional rabbit hopping away from the road. Only the richest of the rich live up here, not café bartenders, even if they do look like Ava. The two women in the front seat don't say a word. So I don't either.

We begin passing cars parked on the side of the road. Someone's having a party. Finally we pull into a circular drive of one of those enormous stucco mansions Old Hollywood liked to build. But there's not a peep of music coming from the giant house and the windows are dark too. When we climb out of the car, the whole night is quiet.

I turn to Ava. "Can you at least tell me—"

"Silence," she commands, pulling out a black leather collar and swiftly snapping it around my neck. "You don't talk anymore, understand? Just 'yes, ma'am' and 'no, ma'am' whenever you're asked a question. Your job tonight is to obey me—without question."

Her green eyes blaze. Part of me wants to tell her to fuck off , beautiful or not. I might not be some hardcore BDSM kinkster like some of my friends, but I do know a thing or two about safewords and consent and she hasn't asked me for either. Who's to say I even want to be here? Then I realize that this is the moment she's giving me the choice. To go or stay. Say yay or nay.

"Fine," I say, adjusting the collar. "But I'm leaving anytime I want."

The words sound so weak in the foggy night that her full lips curve into a smile. Then she snaps a leash onto my collar and leads me down a flagstone path, away from the front of the house and down a side lawn to a door that clearly leads to a basement.

At first I can't tell if I'm at a party, a club, a speakeasy or a dungeon.

Maybe it's all four, here in this massive dark space lit faintly by electric torches. As my eyes adjust, I see there are women sprawled on couches, one naked with another woman buried between her legs. Someone else, in the tell-tale short plaid skirt of a naughty schoolgirl, is bent over a desk as another woman takes a wooden paddle to her bare ass. In one far off corner, a group of couches has been gathered around what looks like a black and white home movie.

As my eyes adjust even more to the dark, I can see that some of the women here are famous. Top actresses. Hollywood studio wives. Tabloid ingénues. Normally I'm not starstruck but now I'm wondering just what kind of party I'm at. Then a fortyish woman approaches—and past the ruffled hair and square glasses, I recognize another very famous face. This actress won an Oscar a few years back. And here she is, with a cunningly voracious look in her eyes.

"Nice work," she says to Ava after appraising me.

"She's cute, talented, moderately feisty," Ava replies.

Moderately feisty? It burns worse than any direct insult could. I open my mouth to tell her where to go, and then I remember the collar around my neck.

The Oscar winner feels my biceps and runs a hand over my haircut, then lifts my chin like she's buying a horse. "The real thing," she muses. "Let's see the rest of her."

They lead me farther in to where actual stocks have been set up. They secure my head and hands in the stocks—and then they strip me, taking my jeans and underwear down to my ankles and pushing my shirt up to my neck. Multiple hands travel over my body, evaluating me efficiently and thoroughly, their fingers cool on my skin. I've never even had a three-way before, and now I'm letting three, maybe four, strangers touch my naked body. Someone is rubbing my clit, someone else is slipping their finger in my ass. And my passivity is unexpectedly hot. There's no giggling, nervous girl to seduce tonight, I don't have to break out my best moves or monitor and adjust to all of her feelings. I'm just a captive getting efficiently and anonymously stimulated. Succumbing to it, an ocean of euphoria beginning in my scalp and then washing like the surf through my blood. And then yes, someone presses a cool and slippery toy against my hot cunt until an authoritative voice commands:

"No."

That's Ava's voice. I can identify it even in this crowd, as a dog is attuned to his master's command.

She continues, "She doesn't get to come yet. I'll decide when she does."

Goddammit. I twist angrily in my stocks and a sharp hand slaps my right ass cheek. "Oh, was someone hoping to be a lazy little bottom tonight?" Ava says in my ear. "It's not going to be that easy for you—nothing about serving me is."

I'm released and stand up gingerly, wanting to stretch my back, but Ava has another girl quickly pull my shirt off and take it away with my jeans and underwear and shoes. Now I'm naked at a party in just a collar and leash. And the only truly shocking thing is how easily and naturally I've relinquished all control. As two new women come up to feel my ass and coo over my muscles, I know now that my self-concept as a cocky but charming butch lothario is dead wrong, laughably so, because a real butch lothario wouldn't be standing here like a beautiful woman's leashed dog.

The Oscar winner is back and speaking to Ava, who turns and tugs my leash. "Come on."

I'm led through the darkness, past cages, spanking stools and bondage tables. Mentally I'm beginning to adjust. I've heard about BDSM play parties. And that's all this is, I tell myself. Ava heard my slave comment at the restaurant and mistook me for an experienced submissive.

She leads me through a sliding glass door and onto a patio. The cool night feels good on my flushed skin. Then I see Heather from the restaurant. She's sprawled naked on a divan while an older woman goes down on her. The blonde wig is gone and she's back to her pink ponytails, moaning and holding her breasts.

Damp grass under my bare feet, then Ava leads me up stone stairs to a massive pillared pavilion with an outdoor fireplace.

The Oscar winner sits down on one of those wicker loveseat swings and Ava positions me before her.

"You did a wonderful job," Oscar Winner compliments Ava. "She's perfect. Like a beautiful boy turned into a girl."

She's talking about me. Even though *boyish* is the word I normally hear, not *beautiful* and rarely *girl*. And in any case, I don't give a shit what Oscar Winner thinks. I care about pleasing Ava. Who I look pleadingly at now.

Ava glances at me uneasily, then stares off into the dark.

Oscar winner trails filed-down fingernails up my thigh. She's attractive but I can't help recoiling. "Um..." I begin awkwardly.

Oscar Winner frowns. "Apparently you haven't been voice-trained," she says coolly. "You don't speak until spoken to, dear."

I look pleadingly at Ava again. This time she intervenes.

"Actually, she hasn't had much formal training at all," she says. "She's one of my newer finds. Why don't I run her through the basics and bring her to you later."

Oscar Winner's face goes cold. "So all this was for nothing?"

"I'm sorry. I'm really sorry." It's kind of stunning to hear the contrition in Ava's voice. "I thought she would be prepared. It won't take long."

Oscar Winner rises and shrugs, as if I'm just a disobedient puppy she's turning over. "Make it quick, or I'll use one of the others." She vanishes across the grass.

I stare at the stone pavilion floor, bracing for Ava's wrath.

"Good going," she says coldly.

"I didn't know—I'm not part of this scene. I was kidding when I said I was your slave. Why the hell did you even bring me here?"

Ava's heels click across the stone. One fingertip lifts my chin. "Most girls would kill to come to these parties," she snaps. "If you're not submissive, why did you let me collar you?"

"Because it was you. I'd let you do anything to me." The words sound pitiful even to me as soon as I say them.

Her mouth creeps into a tiny smile. "Oh no, you're not submissive at all. Not you."

I shrug sullenly.

She pushes me onto the swing so fast that I topple onto my front. It begins rocking wildly and it's hard to get my balance but I twist around and then Ava is straddling me. "Down!" she commands, looming over me. I obediently stretch out on my back on cushions, ready to welcome her voluptuous weight onto my face. Instead she pinches my nipples hard, twisting them slightly. It hurts a little, but it feels good too. And then she reaches back and begins slapping my clit.

I jump. "Ow!"

"Be quiet. It doesn't hurt."

She's right, it stings more than anything, but I can't help jerking and twisting beneath her as she continues her half-teasing, half-sadistic assault on my nipples and clit. I'm not enjoying this, I tell myself, but my hips are rising with a will of their own to meet her hand and my pussy is wet and aching. I'm just an animal who wants to be fucked right now, and willing to debase myself however I need to make it happen.

She flips me over her lap. She is strong, possibly even stronger than I am which is humiliating and a turn-on at the same time. "Now," she says, giving my bottom a slap, "you're going to be truthful with me." Another slap.

"I've been truthful all night!"

She spanks me harder. "That right there is a lie. Strutting up to me and presenting yourself as my slave, and then I give you the gift of attending this very A-list party and you embarrass me and say you're not submissive…"

"Okay, I am! I am!"

"Am what?"

"A liar. A submissive. Your slave."

The spanking continues. She's touching my nipples too, which are extra-sensitive from the earlier pinching and my clit is rubbing against her satin dress, and I am pretty much one howling, writhing mass of submissive hunger on her lap. Then something new comes down on my ass, something rubbery. She's brought the toy from earlier.

"Yes, I know you want this," she says, smacking it against my ass twice, then a third time. "You're such a greedy little bottom, I can tell you are going to need lots of work. Lots of training..."

And she says some other things, but I don't hear them because the toy is pushing into my grateful pussy and I am spreading my legs without shame. Nothing has ever felt as good as her silicone cock inside me and her fingernails on my inflamed ass while I grind out my love on her satin dress. She keeps fucking me, spanking me, degrading me, until I'm coming and coming all over her dress in ecstatic wet waves.

"You filthy little sub," she says when I'm done, shoving me down to the cold stone floor. "Look at what you did to my gown."

"I'm sorry."

"Not as sorry as you will be. Get on your knees." She positions me in front of her. "I'm going to train you. And you're going to be a very good student, understand? I'm the one who owns you now."

I nod and kiss her feet to show my obedience. The fog is moving through the pavilion and I'm shivering. A drift of voices moves past us, women who sound like they're looking for us. Ava goes tense and I stay quiet. But the darkness and the fog keep our secrets and the voices fade. It's going to be just us then. Which is how I want it. I bury my face in her dress and her fingers begin to move through my hair, tracing my ears, stroking my neck. Opening a door in my mind to a universe of destinations reigned over by a darkness shaped like her.

THE NOSE ART GAL
Mary Tintagel

THE B-17 VECTORED DOWN INTO THE DRY LAKE BED AND TOUCHED DOWN, blasting clouds of salt dust into the air as its wheels kissed Mother Earth. The girls had done a beautiful job on it. It was probably in better condition now than it had been over the skies of Europe undertaking daylight raids back in '44. Janey smiled to herself as she saw the obviously re-painted nose art on the starboard side. It was too daring to be a design by Esquire artist George Petty. The depiction of a naked muscular Amazon with jutting conical breasts did not match straight tastes, and she seriously doubted that the original name of the bomber had been 'Queen Bitch.' That sounded like the sense of humor of the ship's owner and pilot, Sally 'Big Sal' Burroughs, one of the foremost restorers of vintage aircraft in the country. She was a rich woman and, as far as Janey knew, she got whatever the hell she wanted. As the engines died the belly-hatch popped and Big Sal dropped down onto the salty dirt. Janey had only ever seen her at air shows prior to this, but she always seemed to be dressed exactly the same—totally authentic Women Air Force Service Pilot's uniform—aviators, helmet, flying jacket and olive drab flying suit.

"Hi, baby," greeted Big Sal. "Glad you could make it. No second thoughts?"

"Actually, I'm scared witless. Who wouldn't be? But I've had it with indoor skydiving and ice baths. I wanna do it for real," Janey stated with an odd mixture of fear and feistiness.

"Come take a look on the port side of the ship," ordered Big Sal.

The nose art on this side was very freshly painted. Janey could tell that because one of the figures was based on self-shots she's taken with her phone and e-mailed to Big Sal only last week. The picture of Janey was beautiful, long limbed and naked, apart from a length of chiffon that snaked across her breasts and down her belly. However, the image of Janey was not alone on the fuselage; the 'Queen Bitch' Amazon from the starboard side was directly behind her—grinding into her—fucking her with a strap-on, presumably.

"There's no turning back even if you wanted to," smiled Big Sal. "Get in the ship."

Janey locked her 4x4 and walked back toward the bomber. What on earth had she been thinking signing up for something like this with virtual strangers? Would Big Sal really have forced her into the B-17 against her will? There was little point worrying about it now. She climbed up into the bomber and moved forward to the cockpit where Big Sal introduced her to Celia and Kate who would be doing the piloting on this 'mission.' For obvious reasons, Big Sal was going to be indisposed.

Within a few minutes the four engines had roared to life again and the plane was bumping down the makeshift runway; then it bucked upwards and soared high into the azure Nevada sky. In the far distance Janey could see Vegas. It was another 48 hours until she was expected at her shift in the show at the MGM Grand. She wondered if she would be in any fit state to make it. Big Sal disappeared shortly after takeoff and returned a little while later having changed into a blue skydiving suit. The chute was already on her back, and on her chest dangled the straps of a dual-jump harness. Well, there was no point being coy. Janey stripped off and put her belongings and clothes in the plastic bag Big Sal handed her. Next, she applied lubricant from an oversized white tube—working it up all the way inside herself—more or less filling her whole cunt with it, as Big Sal had instructed. Finally, the big woman took hold of her and guided her into the harness. There was something comforting about the closeness, the feel of Big Sal's arms around her. She had wanted this. It was the ultimate danger-fuck. The ultimate ecstasy in the face of death; if only she could overcome her fear and doubts— as well as the hit and run urge to be violently sick that was strobing in the pit of her stomach.

"It's time, honey," Big Sal whispered directly into her ear, and then they were through the hatch and out into the yawning blue. The desert floor rolled and spun beneath them. The wind tore at Janey's eyelids and genitals like a set of invisible claws. Her labia were forced violently open, the air itself was raping her, forcing the lubricant hard up against her aching cervix like a plug of iron. Worse still was the effect on her breasts, they were flattened like pancakes against her. Tissue and membrane oscillated constantly and painfully. Her nipples insisted on maintaining their erectness and they now looked and felt like lumps of raw steak. The cold was infinitely worse than in the preparatory ice baths. She had thought that 'frozen to the marrow' was just a turn of phrase, but now she was all too conscious of the cold seeping deep into her bones.

Then it happened. Big Sal let her loose from the harness. She had known it was going to happen, but that certainly didn't help. She was thousands of feet up, naked and falling helplessly without a parachute. She rolled over and splayed her legs as wide as she could, then gripped her ankles. Above her was Big Sal, swooping down like a hawk. Big Sal had been wearing a special skydiving suit manufactured in sections connected by zippers. She had removed the sleeves and leggings, as well as the upper part of the chest section. Even under attack from the screaming wind, her tits were magnificent, and crested with diamond hard nipples. Her own hair was half blinding her, but then Janey saw it—a strap on dildo poking out of the crotch of Big Sal's suit. Dear God. Glinting in the sun it looked as big as a missile. There was no way.... At terminal velocity the bulbous head of the dildo whacked into Janey's inner thigh. There would be the bruise to end all bruises tomorrow. Then it rebounded into her snatch. The impact was like a shotgun going off inside her. Her vaginal muscles clamped down on the intruder, and Janey screamed in agony until she realized that she was having the most powerful orgasm she had ever experienced. Every single muscle in her stomach and abdomen seemed to be involved. It was the sweetest and most intense feeling. She grabbed at Big Sal and crushed her nearer in a vain effort to prolong it, but the feeling subsided all too quickly.

Big Sal thrust into her only ten or a dozen times before the next climax. There was so little time now. Every moment of the freefall seemed precious. Big Sal withdrew and then turned Janey around in the air, inverting her. Then she strapped her in place so they couldn't be separated. Big Sal's face was pushed so hard into her crotch it felt like part of her. Big Sal was merciless; not just tonguing but biting the hood and lips hard. Too hard. Janey screwed her eyes shut. Not just against the pain, the wind was now unbearable. Why hadn't Big Sal allowed her to wear goggles? But at least now, with her eyes closed, she couldn't see the ground barreling up towards them. Blindly, she reached for the strap-on attachments and started tugging at them. She wanted to detach the strap-on and do something to Big Sal—pleasure her, hurt her, anything—this had all just been a one way street so far, but her hand was brutally slapped away. Now Janey was being released from the harness again, and it felt like some sort of punishment for her attempt to touch Big Sal. But Big Sal was only refitting Janey into her original position—the typical tandem jumping position. Janey was aware that her anus was now cupping the tip of the dildo. She thought she knew what was coming next, but she was wrong. Big Sal pulled the ripcord on her harness and the chute deployed above them in a sudden blossoming of white silk. The deceleration drove the strap-on up her rectum like a piledriver, practically filleting her, or so it felt. There was nothing akin to pleasure, just a sense of injury and defilement—yet still she wanted it. Big Sal—the Queen Bitch—had wanted to hurt her and she had. The pain unlocked every corner of her mind. Images and memories, long, long forgotten and suppressed came to the forefront of Janey's consciousness—her first crush, at age twelve; and further back, like dinosaur bones uncovered by desert wind—impossibly early recollections of sucking hard at her mother's breast.

As the ground loomed nearer her normal thought processes were kick-started and then preoccupied with a single concern; what was going to happen when they hit the ground? Janey couldn't absorb the impact of the landing with bare feet—the plan had been for her to put her feet on Big Sal's boots, but if the Queen Bitch absorbed the momentum Janey's ass would be impaled even further. Now, she enjoyed pain, but that would be too much. Too much for anyone. Janey engaged in more futile fumbling, reaching back to somehow pull the strap-on out, but Big Sal was pressed right up against Janey by virtue of the harness and her own seemingly inexhaustible and irresistible strength. Big Sal's left arm was tight around Janey's belly. Big Sal's right hand was roving all over, paying particular attention to the naked girl's tits. These weren't loving caresses—it was more like backseat groping at a drive-in. And then Janey realized, she'd been ridden until she was broken, like a horse at a rodeo. Her will had drained away like melted snow. She wanted to please her dominant, to offer herself to her completely, but she had to bargain with her; she had to find a way to avoid the injury she might sustain on impact. Janey arched her body until she was whispering in Big Sal's ear; she didn't know what the Queen Bitch heard and what she didn't. She just kept talking. She offered eternal worship and forever love—a thousand kinds of bullshit, a thousand more promises that she could never keep. As the ground approached Janey was starting to believe her own lies. There would be only Big Sal for her now. She would forget all the others. She would forget Carla, the 'love of her life' who had dumped her so mercilessly. She would forget Siri at the show—she had planned to make a move on her soon. She and Big Sal would live in a ranch house not far from an airfield and Janey too would learn to fly a B-17. She wouldn't just be a nose art gal, she would be a real pilot—just like the women who had lived and died transporting bombers around for the Air Force during the War.

Reality chomped hard on her awareness. She was only forty feet above the ground and she still had the motherfucker of a dildo up her. She placed her feet on top of Big Sal's boots. If she didn't, her feet would probably break, or at least have the soles sliced to ribbons. She braced herself mentally and physically for the worst. The worst did not arrive. Big Sal knew when to exercise sexual mercy. Janey understood, too. The broken horse could be ridden again and again. But dear God, not like this again. A warm bed and a goddamn drink was what she needed, a stiff drink.

The landing was expert and Janey scarcely felt a thing. She stood under the blazing sun, yet she was so chilled that hypothermia would be a possibility. Big Sal put her over her shoulder like the proverbial rag doll and started walking. A crosswind had caused them to miss the landing point by about eight hundred yards, and the Queen Bitch apologized for this. Actually apologized. There was a tent at the landing site and the promise of comforts within.

"You're a good sport, baby," judged Big Sal. "I know it isn't easy the first time and I know I'm kinda rough, but it's just who I am. I never learned to be gentle."

"You're amazing—but frankly, you're also fucking certifiable," Janey managed to laugh. "How many times have you done that now?"

"Well, I guess it depends how you count it. Five times, I suppose. But I never released a girl from the harness until today. I wasn't sure if it would work but it was actually easier than I thought."

"What the Hell?" mouthed the girl, concerned, somewhat shocked. She'd signed up for the ultimate danger-fuck, and received it with a vengeance. Now they had arrived at the tent—a big army surplus field tent.

Once inside, Big Sal wrapped Janey in a thermal blanket and poured her some hot coffee from a thermos. There was a period of shaking and shivering before her body's temperature regained its normal equilibrium. Janey was offered candy bars to gnaw on to boost her blood sugar levels and took them eagerly. Big Sal reclined on a bed roll after sloughing off the remnants of the flight suit, as well as the dual-harness and strap-on. Janey realized that now Big Sal was naked, she was seeing her properly for the first time. In her own way, she was beautiful: the smoky grey eyes, the aquiline nose, that wide slash of a mouth, the huge and heavy augmented tits, the belly that was hard and muscular (most things about the Queen Bitch were hard one way or another). The mons veneris had been shaved within memory, but was now decorated with a coarse and stubbly growth of black spikiness, a gaudy and unnecessary piercing involved what was obviously a real diamond, not much smaller than a thimble. Janey laughed a little, inwardly—it wouldn't do to laugh at Big Sal. Janey had never really gone in for tattoos. Wasn't there something in the Bible forbidding them? The tattoo on Big Sal was a doozy. It would have been particularly forbidden, probably enough to put Janey's church-going mother into cardiac arrest. Roughly across the top of Big Sal's bikini line, as big as the masthead of a newspaper, and in similar gothic script, it was both an order and a proclamation: *Fuck Me Now*.

Janey kissed Big Sal's belly delicately and then reached for the abandoned strap-on. In response, the big beautiful Amazon rolled onto her belly and spread her legs, and then her buttocks.

"Your choice, baby, but get on with it," Big Sal ordered.

Janey took her time; there was no hurry, as far as she was concerned. Proper tribute, proper worship, took time—when she had finished with the Queen Bitch, she would never want any other girl again.

UNCHARTED TERRITORY

Evan Mora

SHE CALLS ME AT 10:38 IN THE MORNING, AT WORK.

"I want your ass," she says.

That's all she says, all she has to say. It's not a question, and there's nothing for me to say except *yes*, so I do.

Hang up the phone. Make excuses. Meaningless words forgotten as soon as they're spoken. It's possible that someone will ask me about my so-called emergency tomorrow, but I don't care. This is what she does to me.

Sitting on the streetcar, head against the window, the slow west-to-east trundle drives me mad. I feel it already—the urgency, the need. The ache that starts in my cunt and radiates outward until my hands shake like a junkie who's past due for a fix. And I am. It's been more than a week. Long enough for the tenderness in my limbs to recede and my bruises to turn from purple to yellowish green, long enough for one ache to be replaced by another. That's part of it, I know. Part of the game that we play that is not a game at all. She makes me wait because I don't want to wait; because it's another way she can make me suffer.

My stomach flip-flops when we lurch to a stop across from her building. I clutch the upturned collar of my peacoat together at my throat in a vain effort to keep the cold January winds at bay, shivering as much with apprehension as from the temperature. It's an unsettling counterpoint to the arousal thrumming through me, this nervous thread of fear. Today will be different. She's been preparing me for this, has been from the start, but the knowing doesn't make it any easier. She doesn't want to spank me or sink her teeth into my ass—she wants her cock buried deep inside what, for me, is uncharted territory.

17

"Come in, boy," she says by way of greeting, turning to walk back toward the living room and leaving me to close the door and trail after her, the faint scent of her lavender perfume teasing my senses.

"Well?" she says, seating herself regally in a leather wingback chair, crossing her legs above the knee, her black pencil skirt rising a tantalizing inch higher on her smooth, tanned thigh. She is an imposing woman, from the top of her salon styled dark tresses down to the tips of her perfectly manicured toes—but it goes so much deeper than that. She has the kind of presence that inspires devotion and commands obedience. My devotion. My obedience. I swallow hard.

I undress under her impassive gaze, heart hammering in my chest. Tie, dress shirt, binder. These are the first to come off, folded neatly and placed in a pile on the floor. My nipples crinkle into hard points of arousal and I blush to the roots of my short-cropped hair. Shoes, belt and trousers follow, and then all that remains are my snug boxer briefs. I draw a fortifying breath, then push them down and off in a single motion, lying them on the top of the pile.

The transition is the hardest part. Out there, in the world, my image is one of strength and confidence; but in here, with her, there is no room for imagery, only the most basic truth, stripped and exposed. The silence is deafening. I wish she would say something. Order me to kneel, tell me to come to her—anything. But she doesn't. Not yet. She just looks at me. I try hard not to fidget, not to cover my sex, not to let her see how she makes me tremble.

"Come here," she says finally, and I nearly stumble in my haste to get to her, relieved by the comforting familiarity of sitting at her feet. She strokes my hair idly and I rest my head against the side of her leg, kiss the skin there softly. She pulls my head back sharply.

"I didn't tell you to kiss me, boy," she says.

"I'm sorry, Mistress." I murmur. Her hand fisted into my hair feels amazing and my clit jumps at the little hurt. She shakes my head gently before letting go.

"Liar," she says with a hint of affection. "We'll deal with that later, Kai. In the meantime," she continues, "I want you to tell me how your assignment is progressing."

My assignment.

"It's progressing well, Mistress," I stammer, my cheeks reddening again.

Mistress Alessa told me when we met that she expected all of me to be available to her whenever she wanted. When she found out I'd never engaged in any kind of ass-play before, she'd smiled with delight, "Why, that's my very favorite thing!" she'd exclaimed. Penetration in general wasn't high on my list—I preferred to be the one *wearing* the cock—but in short order I found myself fucking her while her finger was pressed deep into my ass, and then, after a spanking that set my skin aflame and had me on the verge of orgasm, I was over her knee with her fingers pumping my ass, crying out and coming shamefully on her lap, tears streaming down my face. She'd sent me off that day with a fat anal plug and instructions to masturbate myself to orgasm every night with the plug deep in my ass.

"You've been practicing every day?" she presses.

"Yes, Mistress." I think even the tips of my ears are blushing.

"Excellent," she says. "Go upstairs and get ready for me."

Just like that? I pad quickly and silently across the hardwood floors and up the stairs to her master suite, my stomach a jumble of nerves even as my sex pulses insistently between my legs.

I stop short at the side of her bed. I know how she wants me: face down, shoulders on the bed, ass raised. There are pillows piled neatly in the centre of the bed with a towel draped over them to place under my hips, but that's not what has me frozen in place. There's a leather hood lying next to the pillows with only a thin slit for a mouth and what looks like a leather blindfold snapped over any eyeholes it might have.

I break out in a cold sweat. I can't do it. I can't pick up this hood and calmly put it on. I'm a wreck just thinking about offering up my ass to this woman, and she's got me so tied up in knots I'd do just about fucking anything for her. But this? It's too much.

"Is there a problem, boy?" Her voice is so close to my ear I jump and then the words just spill out.

"Yes Mistr— I mean *no* Mistress— I'm sorry Mistress...I can't..." I'm wringing my hands, imploring her to understand, my whole body trembling.

She grabs me by the neck and pushes me down.

"Brace yourself," she says in a clipped voice, and I bend forward, forearms on the bed, ass pushed out toward her. I press my face into the mattress, squeezing my eyes shut against the stupid tears that spring up and then the first lash lands, a slash of heat and pain across

19

the centre of my ass that rocks me forward and has me biting my lip to keep from crying out.

She wields the leather strap expertly on my tender skin, covering my ass and my shoulders, and then the more sensitive skin on the top of my thighs until I am crying out, tears falling in earnest, awash with misery and pain.

And then, just as suddenly, it stops. Chest heaving, I suck in deep open-mouthed breaths, knowing better than to move without her say so, acutely aware of the heat emanating from my aching flesh. I hear her moving about behind me, but I'm unprepared when her fingers slip between my legs and into my cunt, and my breath catches in my throat with a gasp.

"Oh, you like that, don't you, boy?" She whispers against my ear, pumping in and out of me slowly, then drawing her slick fingers forward to tease my clit. I'm so hard it's almost painful and I whimper, hips rocking forward helplessly when she pulls my hood back and strokes my length between her thumb and forefinger. Her soft laughter caresses my neck as her fingers dance out of reach.

"So eager to come, and yet when I send you up here to get ready for me, I find you dithering about at the side of the bed." I moan against the coverlet as her fingernails scrape across my ass and she gives me a hard pinch.

"I told you before boy that *all* of your holes belong to me, didn't I?" she says.

"Yes, Mistress." I gasp as she pinches me again.

"Perhaps you need a reminder to help you remember that in future, hmm?" She purrs, delivering a sharp smack with her hand.

"Yes, Mistress!" I cry.

She kicks my feet wider apart, and then her pelvis is snugged up against my ass and the cool head of her cock slips into my cunt. I grunt into the mattress as she grabs my hips and pulls me back toward her, impaling me fully on her shaft. She fucks me deep and rough, hips slapping against my hot ass, then she leans forward, draping her torso across my back and slipping one hand around to squeeze my neck while she continues to fuck me, slowly cutting off my ability to breathe, the pressure in my head and my clit rising to critical levels.

"You belong to me, boy," she breathes into my ear. "Whenever, and however I like." She sinks her teeth into the hollow between my shoulder and neck, biting down so deeply that stars explode behind my eyelids and I cry out and come so hard I think for a moment that I might pass out.

She eases her weight off of me, releasing her grip on my throat and withdrawing her cock while I half-lie on the bed, panting like a dog, waiting for my vision to clear and wondering whether my legs will hold me if I try to stand up. I needn't worry though, because she orders me to kneel, and I sink gratefully to the floor at her feet.

"You really are incorrigible, aren't you?" She looks at me critically. "First you disobey me when I tell you to get ready for me, and then you come like a teenage boy without so much as asking me first." She tisks disapprovingly. "I'll have to add that to your list of transgressions, but we'll deal with that later. For now, I want to see if you can suck my cock without disgracing yourself any further."

"Yes, Mistress!" I say quickly, rushing on my knees to take up position before the purple cock glistening obscenely between her thighs. She picks up the leather strap in one hand and grasps the base of her cock with the other, slapping it wetly against my face while I chase it like an open-mouthed baby bird. She laughs at my eagerness, but takes pity on me and slides it into my mouth, further than I'm expecting and I gag, reaching out instinctively to grab her thighs. It's the wrong thing to do, and the strap falls smartly against my shoulder.

"Hands behind your back, boy," she says sharply. I quickly fold them behind me, moaning around her cock, the only apology I can offer with my mouth stuffed full like it is. With one hand she holds my head still so she can fuck my mouth, while the other wields the strap again, letting it fall rhythmically against my shoulders, left then right, in a way that feels almost like a caress. I moan again, with pleasure, losing myself in the myriad sensations flooding my senses.

"What a sweet little cocksucker you are, boy," she murmurs, and my clit pulses hard at the slight huskiness in her voice, a telltale sign of her pleasure. I'd suck her cock until my jaw ached if it pleased her, but all too soon she's pulling out, pulling me up by my hair and leading me back to the bed.

"You know what I love about you, boy?" she says, stroking my cheek gently. "I love how pain softens you, how it opens you up..."

She lays the strap down and picks up the hood, and I can't help but stiffen up again.

"Turn around," she says, and I turn away from her, heart hammering in my chest all over again, nervous sweat breaking out on my palms. She slips the hood over my head and laces it up snugly in the back. With the blindfold covering the eye sockets, I'm engulfed in blackness and I feel like I'm on the verge of hyperventilating when her soothing voice calls me back to her.

"Shhhhh...be calm, boy," she whispers next to my ear. "There's nothing to be frightened of." Her nails are tracing sensual patterns across my back and chest, circling the hardened points of my nipples, dipping down to scrape along the sensitive skin of my inner thighs. I shiver uncontrollably, goose bumps breaking out on my skin.

"Feels good, doesn't it?" she says. I nod my agreement, my breathing slowing to something closer to normal. "I just want you to relax; really focus on the sensations in your body, okay?" I nod again.

She guides me onto the bed, positioning me on the pillows so that I'm where she wants me. I'm hyper aware of everything—the softness of the leather against my face; the coarser texture of the towel beneath my hips; the way my nipples just barely brush against the coverlet; the way the mattress dips when she moves into position between my thighs.

I moan softly when her fingertips feather lightly across my ass, and again when she spreads my cheeks apart, exposing me more completely than anyone has before. There's the pop of a bottle top opening, and I gasp as cold lube is drizzled onto my asshole. On the exhale it becomes a moan again as her finger gently circles my anus, dipping inside, spreading the lube thoroughly inside and out, sending frissons of pleasure through me. She works me well, fitting my ass with a plug and letting me have her cock in my cunt again, reaching around to work my clit, bringing me all the way to the peak again and releasing me with a soft command.

"Come for me now, boy." She says, and I'm coming in a perfect void of pleasure, spasming against her fingertips, her cock, the plug filling my ass.

And when I am emptied and relaxed, floating in the darkness inside my hood, she brushes the head of her cock against my ass, then slowly presses forward. It's bigger—so much bigger than the plug I've become accustomed to—that my muscles instinctively tense again, despite her gentle foray.

"Relax boy, just relax..." she whispers softly.

And I try, I really try, repeating the word over and over to myself, but as the head of her cock disappears into my ass I think briefly, desperately, that I can't do this, that the pain is too intense. My hands clench into white knuckled fists gripping the sheets and my safeword dances behind my eyelids and brushes against my tongue as pain knifes through my body. I try to breathe through it—I don't want her to be disappointed in me when this is so clearly what she wants...

But then a curious thing happens. As she slowly thrusts more deeply into my ass, the pain lessens, and exquisite sensations rise up to mingle with the pain. She's slowly but gradually increasing her pace, and sweat breaks out all over my body. My hips rise up to meet each thrust and I'm breathing open-mouthed moans into the bed in time to the rhythm of her fucking me. She's making breathy sounds of her own, and I can feel her pleasure rising and I am lost, completely engulfed in sensation, sinking into it, time and place disappearing until there is only Her. Pleasing Her. Giving myself over to Her. She cries out suddenly, her body tensing above me as she reaches her peak, and I feel a pleasure, a *gratitude*, so intense that it transcends orgasm completely.

In the aftermath, I am still floating, only vaguely aware of her cleaning me, removing my hood and urging me to lie down beside her. Gradually, the sensation begins to ebb, and she kisses me deeply, exploring my mouth leisurely with her tongue, biting my lip almost playfully.

"What a delight you are, boy," she says.

"In fact," she continues, unbuckling her harness and laying her strap-on to the side, revealing the glossy dark triangle beneath; the swollen glistening folds, "I think you've earned yourself a reward."

And I rush to take my place, the swell of gratitude returning to fill all the space in my chest, as I determine to show her just what a good boy I can be.

GRACE: UNDER PRESSURE

D. L. King

"WHEN I RECALL HER, I THINK OF HER AS A QUEEN. I KNOW, IT SOUNDS stupid—sappy, even. It's just the way I've always seen her, you know?"

"Like a queen. Like Queen Elizabeth, you mean?"

"No, don't be ridiculous. Well, maybe like Elizabeth I."

"So she's old."

"No. Elizabeth I wasn't always old, you know; people aren't born old. I just mean regal. She had a very regal bearing. It was the sense I got the very first time I saw her, back in college."

"She was a prof? Kinky."

"No, she was a student. If you want to hear the story just shut up and listen." I gave her nipple a pinch.

Toni yipped and cast her eyes down. "Okay, I promise; I'll be good. Tell me."

I doubted it.

"It was freshman year. I went away to school and didn't know anyone there. My resident adviser took his job seriously and wanted the people on his floor to be comfortable and feel at home. The day before classes began, he knocked on my door and said he had someone he wanted me to meet. Said he thought we'd get along." Telling Toni the story brought it all back.

ఆఈ

HE'D ASKED ME TO JOIN HIM FOR LUNCH AND WE WENT DOWN TO THE cafeteria. We joined the line and got our food and as I followed him to a table, my eye was drawn to a woman sitting alone in the middle of the room. Even then, I noticed her perfect posture. As she leaned

25

her head back to take a drink from her bottle of water, our eyes met. She held my gaze and didn't pull away. I was the one who dropped eye contact. Regal was the word that came to mind, even then. An air of quiet power.

I was a little shocked when John led me to her table and put his tray down. "Mina," he said, "this is my friend, Grace. She's the sister of my best friend back home. I thought you guys might get along."

I put my tray down opposite her and smiled. "Hi," I said.

"Hello Mina." She smiled back. Her eyes were the most amazing dark blue. I'd never seen anything like them. She had long, straight, dark hair. She wore no makeup, as far as I could tell, but then, she didn't need any. She was wearing a Laura Ashley style sundress with spaghetti straps.

I was instantly comfortable and on edge, at the same time. We talked and found out we had a lot in common: we liked the same music, read the same books, liked the same art—it was like we were made to be friends. I don't know if John really thought we'd be friends, or if he'd promised his friend that he'd look after his sister, but there was an immediate attraction.

We didn't have any classes in common. I'd come as an art major but Mina was a psychology major. She said she'd originally applied to be an art major and her portfolio had gotten her almost a full ride, but she really didn't want to major in art. She wanted to know what made people tick. She wanted to be a therapist. I wondered if she'd get to keep her scholarship.

That first week, I saw her with a bunch of different guys and girls. Everyone seemed to hang on her every word. One night she came by my room—specifically to meet my roommate. It was then I figured I didn't have a chance. But about two weeks into classes, she sought me out for lunch again. "Let's have dinner tonight," she'd said. "I know this place downtown. It's cheap but really good. You like Ethiopian food, don't you?"

"Sure," I'd replied. I'd never had Ethiopian food. But I definitely wanted to spend time with her. Later, after classes, we took a bus downtown to a little hole-in-the-wall place. We were the only customers. It was still early, I thought. It would get crowded later.

It never did.

The food was all right. I wasn't all that impressed. We ate and talked about classes and music. I asked if she was going out with anyone, mentioning that I'd seen her with this guy, or that girl. She refused to comment, except to say they were all very nice people. After dinner, we took the bus back to campus and she walked me to my room. She kissed me and it was like my world exploded. And then it literally did. I turned frightened eyes to her and rushed into my room, slamming the door behind me, flew into the bathroom my roommate and I shared with the girls next door and was immediately, violently sick.

After everything was out of my stomach and I had crawled to my bed, I realized what I'd done. God, she probably thought the kiss had freaked me out. Now what was I going to do? But no, maybe she'd gotten sick too. It wasn't that I wanted her to be sick, but if she was, she'd probably figure out what happened.

My roommate came home a short time later and I pleaded with her to find Mina and tell her I was sick. She agreed and left—right before I passed out. I woke up the next morning, still fully dressed and on top of the covers on my bed. My first thought was

Mina. My second thought was that I seemed to feel okay. I got up, showered, threw on some jeans and went to find Mina. She was in the cafeteria, eating lunch.

"Are you okay?" she asked. "Your roommate said something about you throwing up all over the place."

"I am now. It must have been the food," I said. "Are you okay?"

"No, I'm fine. I didn't get sick at all. Maybe it was a psychosomatic reaction," she said pointedly.

"No, I don't think so. I think it was something I ate because... wait, what are you, um, no, you were right last night, I like girls, I mean, if that's what you mean."

"If you say so." She gave me an appraising look, from my head to my toes, pausing at my waist and then back up to my eyes. "And what is it you think you want?" she said.

She seemed to be waiting for an answer but I wasn't sure of the context. A lot of thoughts circled my mind: Friendship. You. Sex. Pain. Sex. You. But I said, "To make you happy." I hoped it was the right answer.

She looked at me for a minute, then kissed me on the nose. "I'll call you," she said, then turned and walked away.

Oh, shit; wrong answer. I was going to pine over her, just like that straight cheerleader in high school. I knew I would and I knew there was nothing I could do about it. I'd already gotten myself all worked up over her. Classes dragged and I stopped eating in the cafeteria, bringing the food back to my room, instead. I didn't want to see her reject me.

About a week later, I was in my room eating a tuna sandwich when there was a knock at the door. I opened it and Grace was standing there, vintage poodle skirt, white sweater, with her hands on her hips.

"Where have you been?" she said. "I know your schedule and you haven't been down to eat in days. What is your deal?" She pushed her way into the room and saw my sandwich on the desk. "Why are you eating in your room? Are you trying to avoid me?"

I was speechless. I think I just looked at her with my mouth open.

"Well?" she said, staring at me.

Oh, an answer—she wanted an answer. "Well, I...I mean, I could tell you weren't interested and, I just really didn't want to..." My words faded away. Everything sounded lame.

"Listen, Mina, I'll tell you when I'm not interested." She grabbed my arm and twisted it behind my back, kicked the door closed with her foot and kissed me. I mean really kissed me. She took my breath away. And just as quickly and violently as she initiated the kiss, she stopped kissing me. She drew me over to the bed and pulled me over her lap. She yanked my shorts down and began to spank me. "I waited and waited," she said as she thrashed my bottom over and over, "and I never caught a glimpse of you after I kissed you in the hall."

I reached around to cover my butt because the spanking really hurt. She grabbed my hand and twisted it up with the other one and held them together at the small of my back.

"Don't you dare." Her voice was low and dangerous and it made me gush. I stopped moving. She reached between my legs and ran her hand over my pussy, up to my anus. "Oh, so that's the way it is, is it?"

I detected a smile in her voice, though I couldn't see her face.

"Where's your roommate?"

"Um, she's, um..." Three more smacks rained down.

"Where is she?"

"Class. She has a class," I yelped.

"Good." She ripped my underwear down my legs and buried two fingers in my cunt. They pressed insistently against my G spot. "This is mine now," she said. She pumped them in and out before circling my clit. "And this is mine," she said. "Stay." She took her hand away from my wrists and though my arms were strained and sore from the position, I kept them there. She opened my legs and placed my outside foot on the floor, then moved it up toward my head, spreading me open. I was so wet, I was dripping. "You do not presume to know what I'm thinking, especially when we've just met. Is that clear?"

"Yes, Grace," I said. I felt the palm of her hand smack against my wet, open pussy and yelped.

"Not a sound," she threatened, and proceeded to smack my pussy over and over. "Let this be a warning to you."

She continued to admonish me, but I'd lost the train of thought. Without my volition, my body humped against her hand as it landed. My breaths came faster and shorter as the rhythm of her spanks doubled, or even tripled, each one seeming to land harder than the one before. Just before I came, she stopped. She stuffed her index finger inside me, smashed my clit against my body with her thumb and then squeezed hard.

My body tensed and then convulsed against her. I could feel myself flopping around on her lap, bouncing against her knee and grinding into her hand, legs scrabbling for purchase. The orgasm wouldn't stop. It seemed to go on forever, and the pressure of her fingers never let up. Finally the spasms subsided and I lay sprawled over her, no longer moving. She gathered me up and put me on the bed, face up and stared down into my eyes. I willed myself to stare back. She was smiling. "Yeah, I think this is going to work just fine," she said. "We'll go out for dinner on Friday—not the Ethiopian place, someplace safe," she said with a wink. "Then after, you'll come to my room. I have a single. We'll spend some time, you know, getting to know each other. Shave off that bush. I don't like the barrier."

Without another word, she got up and walked out, closing the door behind her. I was left lying on my bed, pants and underwear pulled down around my calves and my t-shirt pulled up to my waist.

We were together for the next four years. It wasn't always like that. We spent a lot of that time studying, going to the movies together, going out to eat, hanging out in the student lounge with friends; normal stuff , you know, but periodically, we'd have some mind-blowing kinky sex. I discovered that whenever Grace felt pressure or stress, she'd take it out on my body, so to speak. If she were tense, she'd play rough. The tenser she was, the rougher she played. And I could be the cause of that tension, I mean, on purpose. I could bring on a play session by my actions. I'm not saying that was a good thing to do, I'm just saying that if I pushed her, I could get what I wanted.

Don't get me wrong, our relationship was based on dominance and submission. I was her dutiful sub and she was my goddess, but she only played fl at out, like that, when she was tense. I think it was a way for her to unwind.

She had a corner room and only shared one wall with another room. That person never seemed to be home. I think she had a boyfriend at another school and spent most of her time with him, so, with music on, we could get a little noisy without worrying about it.

I remember one time she'd been working on a paper practically non-stop and had just gotten it in, under the wire. It wasn't the usual way she worked. She was very careful and meticulous and always left plenty of time to get her work done. I chided her about it and she practically ripped my clothes off , tied me to her bed, spread eagle, and slapped, pinched and tortured me for hours.

She used a leather crop on my breasts and pussy before attaching clothespins to my nipples and labia. She had special clothespins, with holes drilled in their wings so she could tie them to things. First she tied my pussy lips open, then she tied the clothespins on my nipples to a plant hanger above her bed, stretching them just enough to keep the tension going. She took turns smacking my open pussy and twisting her fingers inside me until I writhed enough to pull one of the clothespins off my nipple. That's when she took pity on me and fucked me with a vibrator we'd bought together. She took the pins off my nipples, but left the labial pins on. Exposing that tissue to the air for that long can dry it out, you know, but I was so turned on, that never happened.

CRADO

I'D GOTTEN LOST IN THE TELLING—TRANSPORTED BACK TO THAT TIME. Toni hadn't interrupted me in a long time. I refocused on what I was doing. She was sort of glassy-eyed. Her mouth was open and she was panting to the rhythm of my palm gently smacking her shaved pussy, over and over. I'd been doing it throughout my tale and, though I wasn't hitting her hard, her skin was pretty swollen and red.

She was on her back, on my bondage table, in the dungeon. Her wrists were tied over her head and her knees were bent with her feet pushed up almost against her butt. Her ankle cuff s were fastened to the table so she couldn't straighten out. That left her sex gloriously exposed to my ministrations.

"What, no questions?" I said. "You don't want to know anything else?" I ran my index finger through her very slick folds.

She started to close her knees. "Don't you dare or I'll smack you with the crop—a lot harder than I've been smacking you."

"Sorry, ma'am." She spread her knees again. "But, you were a sub? I don't get it."

"Oh, yes, very much so." I leaned down and bit one of her nipples. "It was Grace who discovered my sadistic streak. Our senior year, she started training me as a dominant. She had me practice on a couple of her other submissive friends. It was fun and I found I was good at it." I unfastened one of her ankles and lifted the leg up so I could fasten it to a chain hanging above the table and then did the same with her other leg.

"Keep 'em spread for me." I began fastening my harness. I'd put a medium sized cock in. "What do you think? Do you think I'm good at it?"

"Oh, yes, ma'am. Yes, ma'am, I do."

"Grace and I sort of broke up after graduation. She was a top and she'd made me a top. We didn't really work as a couple anymore. We're still friends, though. And she's the only woman I'll bottom to." Kneeling between Toni's legs, I twisted the plug in her ass and finger fucked her cunt enough to assure myself that she was plenty wet and ready. I kept my palm on the plug's guard as I slowly penetrated her cunt with my cock. Once I was in all the way, I slowly withdrew and repeated the action. I could feel the plug in her ass each time I withdrew.

As I sped up, I circled her clit with my finger. She was close. "So, what do you think?" I said. "Want to meet Grace? She wants to meet you. In fact, she'll be here in about fifteen minutes." I pinched Toni's clit hard and her orgasm took her like a freight train.

THE BULLWHIP & THE BULL RIDER

Sacchi Green

"HEY, WILDCAT, COME WITH ME!"

The throaty female voice would've snared me any other time, but not now. I kicked and thrashed and kept on struggling against the two guys who'd pulled me off my brother Ted. Cindy knelt beside him, all cooing and lovey dovey—Cindy, with her full, smooth curves, who'd been all for a little mutual exploration at last year's rodeo but brushed me off this year and ran to Ted. I'd beat him at bull-riding, beat 'em all! I'd won the trophy belt buckle! But no matter how much I could work like a man, even thrash the men at their own games, their more fleshly rewards were off -limits to me.

Life sucked. My blood was up, the pressure building until I had to explode or die, so I damn sure chose the exploding option. Nobody was gonna hold me back!

Except that the sultry voice came again, much closer now.

"Let me handle her, boys. This calls for a woman's touch."

The calloused cowboy hands trying to hold me back dropped away. Slender satin-clad arms wrapped around me, long dark hair smelling of sweet lemons brushed my cheeks, and my face was pressed against a scarlet blouse that barely covered the peaks of a magnificent pair of breasts. I had the sense to stop struggling.

"Come along with me now, *tigrina*," Miss Violet Montez, lead singer of the intermission entertainment act, murmured into my ear. "I know what you need. And what you don't even know you need."

And, as it turned out, she surely did.

Her trailer was dented and cramped, but I saw right away that it had a narrow built-in bed. She saw me eyeing it.

"Not yet." Her voice turned stern. "Wrangling a bull is one thing. Treating a lady right is something else. Especially your first time."

Well, there wasn't much I could say to that. In fact, I couldn't think of anything to say, and, while I surely knew some things I'd like to do, I didn't know how to go about them with a gorgeous worldly woman like Miss Violet Montez. I'd seen her before at rodeos and such-like gatherings, and fantasized a bit like I did about movie stars and photos in the kind of magazines cowboys tucked under their mattresses in the bunkhouse, but never imagined I'd get this close. "Yes, ma'am," I said, trying to sound polite with just a hint of cocky, but it didn't come out right.

"You sit down in that folding chair and don't stir while I change into something more comfortable." I perked right up at that, but then she added, "and while you wait, give some thought as to whether you want things sweet, spicy, or downright nasty."

I knew my preference, even though I wasn't exactly sure what she meant, but I'd got my brain working enough to know the right answer. "Whatever a lovely lady like you wants is what I want, too."

"We'll just see about that." She scooped up some clothes from the foot of the bed and edged into the tiny bathroom, leaving the door open. I knew better than to get up from my chair, but I did crane my neck to see what I could see. It wasn't much.

The low-necked satin blouse sailed out through the bathroom door, followed by her voice. "Never came across a girl bull rider before in a regular rodeo. Things must be changing for the better."

"Not yet," I admitted. "Not officially. Except at small local shindigs where anything goes." And where my dad was the biggest rancher around and chief sponsor of the rodeo association, but I didn't say that.

Her short black satin skirt with rows of gold spangles followed the blouse, and so did her high-heeled sparkly cowgirl boots and a pair of nylon pantyhose. I wriggled in the chair to see if I could hook that last with my foot, with no luck, but I did get a glimpse of a bare shoulder through the door.

"Well, you can sure handle a bucking bull, but you need to work on self-control, " she said over that shoulder. "And it remains to be seen how much else you can handle..."

"Yes, ma'am." It seemed like the safest thing to say. Now I could see that she was shrugging into a blue-checked shirt, which didn't fit much with my hopeful notions of "something more comfortable."

I looked idly around the trailer. It was dented and shabby, but with colorful pictures on the walls, mostly old rodeo posters, and some fancy duds hanging on hooks, along with...

I only just caught myself from bolting straight up. On one hook, coiled neat as a rattlesnake, hung one of the longest bullwhips I'd ever seen. I looked wildly around again at the posters, and there it was, in a corner of what looked like the oldest one: *Miss Violet Montez, Queen of the Bullwhip.*

I'd seen her way back then! She'd been performing her tricks at the State Fair when I was just knee-high to a fencepost, and she couldn't have been much older than I was now. That'd been the day I'd known for certain that girls could do anything boys could do, and better, if they put their minds to it.

Did she still use the whip? On what? Or maybe who? Some of the racier pictures from those bunkroom magazines came to mind. So did stories from a few paperback books I'd mail-ordered from ads in the back of those magazines. Not enough room in here to swing a whip like that, though. I didn't know whether to be relieved, or disappointed. So many thoughts whirled through my mind that I didn't hear Miss Violet stepping out of the bathroom.

"Like whips, do you?" Her voice, right behind me, made my head swing around so fast my neck cracked.

Right in front of my eyes and nose, close enough that I could tell she didn't shave her private parts but did wash them with lemon soap—though not in the last few hours—was a pair of denim cutoff s so short and tight even Daisy Duke couldn't have got away with them. Looking upward, I saw an expanse of bare midriff topped by the blue-checked shirt, unbuttoned and tied tight under full breasts half-uncovered and straining against such confinement as there was.

I wrenched my gaze upward to her face, trying to tell whether I was being challenged to release those breasts, or even unzip the shorts and give those private parts an airing.

She read my mind. "Don't get big ideas, cowboy. You only get what you earn."

"Yes, *ma'am!*" I'd do most anything for a woman who knew not to call me "cowgirl."

"All right then. You can stand up."

Fast as I stood, she backed up quick enough that I didn't get to brush my own tingling chest against her bountiful one. Then she was sitting on the edge of the bed, one of those high arrangements with drawers underneath to save space. She crossed her long legs, bare all the way up to kingdom come and down to a pair of dusty boots that had seen real work, not like her fancy sparkly ones.

"Now take off your belt."

My belt? With my brand-new shiny trophy buckle? I unbuckled and slid the worn leather out of the belt-loops so fast my split-second of hesitation couldn't have showed. I hoped. She just held out her hands, palms up, and I laid my prize possession across them like an offering.

I was all set to reach for the zipper of my jeans, but she ordered briskly, "Now turn around." I turned.

Faster than I'd got it out, she had the belt back in the loops with the buckle perched between the small of my back and my ass. "Slip your hands down in there right over your butt."

It was awkward, but I did my best, ending up with the backs of my hands right against my skin and the belt buckled around both hips and wrists. I could have wriggled loose, of course, but by then I was bound and determined to please her enough to earn, well, whatever reward there might be. Besides, the feel of my own hands against my butt cheeks, especially if I wiggled my fingers, was tantalizing in an odd sort of way. Maybe soon it would be her hands there. One way or another.

"Turn around again."

I turned. She leaned back a bit. Her shirt looked likely to slip right off one or the other of her breasts, if not both, and I could see the outlines of her nipples poking out like they wanted to speed up the process. It occurred to me that she was enjoying all this a whole lot, which made me enjoy it even more.

"Not bad," she said. "I'll give you a little reward you haven't really earned yet." She stuck out one of her boots and nudged me in the crotch with its toe. "You can clean up my boots."

The boots were even grubbier than I'd noticed at first, with worse things than dust on 'em. Well, so were mine just now, and the crotch of my jeans wasn't much better after riding the bulls. It was getting mighty damp, in fact, which could be a help in the cleaning department. I mounted that boot.

My elbows stuck out enough to give me some balance. Carefully, so as not to put much downward force on her foot, I squeezed my thighs around the stiff leather and moved myself back and forth, first by tilting my hips, then taking tiny steps forward and back. My jeans got a whole lot wetter. My rhythm got faster. The pressure between my legs was building so high I could hardly stand it.

Her face didn't give me any clue as to whether I was pleasing her, but her nipples seemed to be poking out even more, which didn't soothe my state of frantic arousal one bit.

"Self-control, hotshot, self-control," she scolded. "Keep your attention on your work."

That last part sounded so much like my mother you'd think it would dull my urges, and it did for a bit. "Toby, pay attention to your work!" Ma had scolded, time after time. She'd come West as a schoolteacher, a good one, and even after she married my dad she kept on as principal when the area got populated enough to need that big a school. Ted and I had got pretty well-educated in spite of ourselves, even though we tried not to let on. It was a strange feeling to be minding Miss Violet Montez the way I'd never minded anybody since my mother passed away. Strange, but exciting, and that was downright weird.

"Don't slow down! Where's that bull-riding stamina?" She slid her foot free and ground the boot's toe into my denim seam right where it crossed my clit. I jerked and bit my lip to hang on, and dug my knuckles into the flesh of my butt, which made me jerk even harder.

"Time for the other boot, before you run out of steam."

If I got any more steamed up I'd explode all over her trailer. I almost said so. Luckily her other foot creeping up my inseam distracted me. I didn't know whether talking back would bring on a punishment, or make her give up on me, but I sure didn't want to risk the second. I stared down and concentrated on rubbing that second boot with my thighs and crotch. It didn't seem to be getting any cleaner, in spite of how wet I was.

"Ma'am," I said, meekly as I could manage, "I'm afraid my pants are so grubby by now they're just adding dirt to your boot."

"I believe you're right," she said. "I can smell those britches from here, reeking like a cross between a bull pen and a harem full of horny women."

I dared a quick look. Her tight shorts were looking damp at the seam, too. "I could wash up," I offered.

"You just stay dirty until I tell you otherwise! Now pick up those pantyhose and use them to clean my boot."

Pick them up while my hands were still stuck down the rear of my pants? Impossible! Which was likely the point. Punishment was on the way. That was fine with me, but I still did my best to follow orders, hooking the toe of my boot under the pantyhose, kicking them high up in the air, and ducking my head to try to catch them on my neck. Nearly made it, too.

But crooked elbows weren't enough to keep my balance, especially when something, maybe even Miss Violet's other foot, tripped me up. I went down on my knees, hard, my upper body sprawling over her thighs and my face planted right down in her crotch. I tried to act like the wind was knocked out of me, but to tell the truth I was gulping in her warm, rich woman-scent. Miss Violet wasn't fooled. She lurched her hips up, and for a brief second I even got to taste the wetness seeping through her shorts, but then she threw me off onto the floor. It was only when my hands broke the fall that I noticed they'd come out of my pants.

She stood above me, arms crossed over her breasts, a fierce frown on her face that didn't quite go with the gleam in her eyes. "Get up. And get the whip." I got up.

There might have been others in the trailer I hadn't noticed, but I went right for the coil upon coil of the bullwhip. My pants, loose now that my hands were freed from the belt, rode dangerously low on my hips, but I managed to lift down the heavy coils, carry them to her, and loop them over her outstretched hands.

She looked down at the whip for so long I was worried she'd forgotten me. Finally she looked up. "High time this lady got to dance again. It's been too long." That fierce look took hold of her again. "Take off your shirt, go stand right up against the door, and keep your hands raised to the top of it. Surely you can do that much right!"

I did just what she said, not even pausing to straighten out and tighten my belt. Chances were she'd order me to pull the pants down anyway. But for what seemed like a long while nothing happened, except a few sounds of motion behind me like she was looping and relooping the whip. I tried to remember things she'd done with it at the State Fair; hitting targets, flipping fenceposts end over end, sending wagon wheels whirling through the air, even making pictures with its curves and loops high over her head, outlines that looked like ocean waves or a mountain range or even handwriting in some unknown language.

She hadn't used it on living flesh, human or animal, but I had no doubt that she could kill or maim with it if she had a mind to, or just etch lines into skin precisely where she wanted them to go. Maybe even my skin. A shiver, more of anticipation than dread, ran all the way down from my scalp to the soles of my feet.

But nothing happened. "Ma'am," I said finally, when I couldn't bear the wait any longer and my upraised arms were aching, "Miss Violet, please, ma'am, can I look around at you?"

"When I'm good and ready," she said sharply, and before I could draw another breath something lashed out fast as lightning, wrapped around my butt, and jerked my pants down to the floor, belt, underdrawers and all.

"Now," she said, "you can turn around."

I turned and stared. Naked now all the way down, pants tangled around my boots so I couldn't walk if I tried, I should have felt shame, embarrassment, confusion, fear, but something more powerful swept over me. Something like, like...awe, but even stronger.

Miss Violet stood tall, shirt, shorts and boots discarded, naked as I was except for the bands of bullwhip wrapped from one forearm up to where they bound the whip's grip to her shoulder. Shortened like that, there was no more problem with lack of space to swing it. The tightly plaited strips on the outer layer of the thong looked like the patterned skin of some exotic snake, climbing down to her hand that gripped it three feet or so above where the long, narrower fall piece was attached. When she twitched her hand, the thin cord at the end, the "cracker" that makes most of the noise when the whip slashes through the air, looked like the tongue of a snake flickering just before it decided to strike.

There'd been a snake charmer lady at the State Fair, too, in skimpy, gaudy duds meant to look Oriental, with a snake around one arm and another draped across her neck. Miss Violet was as far beyond that sideshow faker as a statue of a Greek goddess is beyond a kewpie doll.

What went before had been some kind of game. Now, however much as Miss Violet's curving hips and full, luscious breasts tipped with jutting brown nipples made me want to fuck and be fucked, I wanted even more to fall on my knees in front of her. To show respect for her greater power and let her use me any way she wanted.

I almost did fall on my knees, but she motioned me to turn back to the door, and I just managed it without stumbling. The whip teased me at first, trickling down my spine, curling around to nip at the sides of my breasts, drifting across my butt cheeks. My legs were as far apart for balance as the pants at my ankles would allow, and when the whip's tip rose up between my thighs to tweak my tenderest parts I jerked so hard I almost toppled backward. In my imagination first it was a real snake, then it was Miss Violet's finger, and I couldn't even tell which made me the wettest.

When the pain came, it was more like ice at first than fire. Thin slices across my shoulder blades, butt cheeks, thighs, too random in the beginning to brace against, accelerating after a while into a storm of strikes that inflamed already-sore places until I felt like I must be red-hot as steel being forged into a blade. A blade to serve Her.

I may have cried. If I did, it wasn't for the pain. The pain was just the means to bring it out. The unfairness of life...of death...Cindy...my mother...the huge, unknown world stretching in front of me...

When the whipping stopped, I didn't know for a while but what it was just another pause. Then Miss Violet's whip-free, snake-free arms came around me from behind, her breasts pressed into my sore back, and she wriggled her cunt against my butt. "You sure stripe up nicely, *tigrina*. Don't worry, hardly any blood. Guess you'd better ride on top tonight, though, for the sake of my sheets."

So I did. Miss Violet was still a goddess, with or without a whip, far better in the glorious flesh than any Greek stone statue. I paid close heed to what made her writhe and cry out with pleasure, and went over the edge a time or two myself when she pumped her knee into my crotch while I was sucking her breasts so hard she yelled but kept hold on my short hair to urge me on.

After a while she showed me just how far my own body could rise above anything I'd ever imagined, spurring pleasure with pain to newer, sharper peaks, until we were both so worn out we could scarcely twitch, and her sheets were soaked with sweat and our mingled juices and the occasional streak of blood after all. Even the leather-bound handle of the bullwhip had come in for some soaking and lay pungently damp beside her pillow.

After a while I asked drowsily, "How come you gave up on your bullwhip act, Miss Violet? You were the best! Doesn't seem as though singing at small-time rodeos would pay better."

She propped her head up on one hand. "There's things men will stand from a young good-looking girl that they won't abide any more when she's a grown woman. You'd find that out soon enough even with bull-riding, so you might as well understand it now. There's a big world out there with chances for you, so don't get stuck here if you can help it."

I didn't want to think about anything but being there with her right that minute, but deep down I knew she was right. When I rode back to the ranch at daybreak, too drained to sort out the remnants of pleasure and pain and smoldering resentment, Daddy was waiting in the barn. He couldn't quite meet my eyes. "Looks like maybe you'd better go back East to school, Toby, the way your Mama always wanted."

"Looks like," I agreed. And that was that. I knew he felt guilty for the way he'd raised me, but I'd never have survived any other way. If he thought going to school back East would teach me proper womanly ways, though, he was dead wrong. Going to a women's college didn't make a lady of me, but I sure learned a lot about women.

And thanks to Miss Violet Montez, whip artiste extraordinaire, I had a good deal to teach, as well.

DEMO MODEL
Rachel Kramer Bussel

EVERYONE GETS BORED WITH SEX AT SOME POINT—EVEN KINKSTERS. Lisa and I had just celebrated our tenth anniversary, having met at an epic play party and instantly recognized each other as compatible souls, in the dungeon and out. It's rare to find a fellow femme who can match me in every way, and I'm extremely grateful we found each other. We were both in our early forties and as devoted as ever, but the spark was starting to die down just a little, enough to unsettle me. I didn't want us to simply settle for lackluster sex or kinky play.

We talked about it but didn't hit on anything until our local dyke BDSM group asked Lisa to teach a class. They wanted her to give the basics on how to debase, degrade, torment and tease a sub, how to keep both parties satisfied, how to make being a top fun and how to draw out a scene. They'd seen us play and Lisa had expressed interest in various domme topics; I suspect they also appreciated the fact that Lisa didn't look mean or stern, but sultry and sexy—or, as I liked to say, she had a butch voice in a femme body. She's six feet tall, curvy, strong and gorgeous. She has short brown hair, and is always trying out new hairstyles. I was busy that night, so they decided to ask someone to demo with Lisa. As it turned out, the woman was a newbie. When Lisa got home that night, the girl—Betty—was all Lisa could talk about. "She had no idea what to expect but she was clearly a sub. She had all these little tells, like when she got on her knees, she bowed without my telling her. She wound up in suspension bondage."

I was starting to get a little sick of hearing about Betty—we're not strictly monogamous, but I still have feelings—when Lisa said that another group at a kinky conference had asked her to do a presentation. We were both attending the all queer women weekend, our first time at this event, held across the country. "What if I was your Betty at the conference?" Lisa gave me a puzzled look, but I was already buzzing with excitement. "Your virgin. I could pretend, roleplay. You could pull me out of the crowd. I'd have to skip my collar and pretend I don't know you the rest of the weekend, but it could be hot. What do you think?"

"*You* want to pretend to *not* be a filthy pervert?" Lisa asked, a grin starting to form on her face. "I don't know if you have it in you." With that, the grin morphed into something far more sadistic as she twisted one of my nipples. I tossed my head back, reveling in the pain, which only made her twist harder. When she slapped my breast hard, the blow made me wet. When she stopped, the first grin was back.

"Okay, I get your point. We both know I'm as kinky as can be, but those people won't know. And maybe it'll give us a way to play a little differently. You can deflower me again and again." Lisa hadn't been my first dominant lover, nor had I been her first sub, though this was the longest relationship either of us had ever been in. I'd never pushed the boundaries of public and private play like I did with her, letting her select outrageously slutty outfits for me, then all but offer me to our waiter or waitress, only to declare myself hers at the end of the night. We'd played at plenty of parties, but we'd also found ways to work our roles into our daily lives.

Maybe that was part of the problem; I was still as in love with Lisa as I'd been ten years ago, but I also, somewhat, knew what to expect. This would be a foray into the unexpected.

We changed our registration, willing to shell out for separate rooms in order to play up our charade. Venturing into a roomful of kinky queer women as a "single" dyke, trying not to make eye contact with Lisa, was a challenge, but I couldn't deny it made me wet. Seeing pretty young things fall all over themselves to talk to her reminded me that my wife was a catch. She was tall and powerful looking; she could work a stare like no one else I'd ever met. But it wasn't just her leather pants or the top she wore, through which anyone could see her large, pierced breasts, or the tattoos she'd designed gracing her arms. It was some special form of charisma she gave off .

We'd agreed that to make the next day's demo more realistic, she would be free to play that night. So would I, but I found myself riveted to Lisa. Seeing her whisper into a beautiful woman's ear didn't make me jealous—it turned me on. I wondered exactly what she'd said that had made the woman dutifully put down her drink and present her hands behind her back to be cuffed with the leather bracelet handcuff s I'd bought Lisa. I knew exactly how they felt, and could guess what this woman felt, standing next to Lisa, waiting for her next instruction.

I kept watching as Lisa took the girl into the play room and made her suck on my wife's nipples, periodically pulling her off so she could give the girl's face a light smack or two. I was so engrossed I hardly noticed the woman who approached me while I unabashedly stared. "You want to try something like that?" I looked up, startled. She was wiry, with a shaved head and lots of freckles. She looked mid-twenties, but could've been my age.

"I'm happy to watch for right now," I said truthfully. "I'm Dawn," I added, offering up the fake name we'd agreed upon, selected since this was the dawn of a new aspect of our relationship—and not too far from my real name, Delia.

"Mel," she said. "And I like to watch." The way she said it sent shivers through me, and I was tempted to extend our conversation into something more, but I resisted. Even the holding off was hot—it made me feel a little bit more like a virgin, waiting for some moment when the stars aligned and I'd know it was right to say yes. I tried to picture myself when I was an actual virgin, someone filled with endless fantasies but not sure how to fulfill them—with women, anyway. If I'd wanted to get some cock, that would've been easy to acquire. But in the town where I grew up, there were only a few girls who liked girls, and, to be honest, they scared me. Little did I know that I liked being scared—safely, that is. Back then I just let my imagination carry me away, and that's what I did as Mel and I watched the scene unfold before us.

The girl, when her mouth was empty, would let out a peal of laughter, then a scream as Lisa found a way to torment her.

Women started handing Lisa toys to use on the girl, everything from a Wartenberg wheel to tease down her back, to a butt plug. I had a feeling Lisa was showing off for my benefit; I was sure of it when she had the crowd count off to fifty smacks of the pretty girl's ass. Eventually I couldn't take it and gripped Mel's hand. "You're fun to watch, too," she whispered. I blushed, shocked at how sexy the simple act of being a voyeur could be. I was so used to being the center of attention I had forgotten the simpler pleasures of play.

⋐⋑

THAT NIGHT, LISA REFUSED TO TOUCH ME WHEN I SNUCK INTO HER ROOM. "If I play with you now, you won't be able to do justice to your demo role tomorrow," she said, cupping my ass tenderly. Tenderness was the last thing I wanted. "I know you, and you don't have a poker face. I want you to squirm for me, to show off this beautiful ass and cry out when I make it nice and red. I want everyone to see you blossom into your kinkiness. Don't you want to do that for me?" When I didn't answer right away, she added, "And for Mel?"

That did it. I ground against the sheets, my clit aching, as I thought about Lisa spanking me and Mel watching, then joining in. Maybe Lisa would let me suck her favorite cock while Mel fisted me. "Yes," I whispered unnecessarily. Lisa knew she had me under her spell.

⋐⋑

THE NEXT DAY, I WORE A VERY SHORT BLACK SKIRT THAT FLARED OUT AT MID-thigh and the barest black lace thong. On top I wore a black t-shirt that said "Bad Girl" across my chest. My outfit felt a little ironic since in fact I was pretending to be far more innocent than I really am, though perhaps my deviousness at having concocted this virginal persona did in fact make me a bad girl.

I stepped into the room and immediately locked eyes with Mel. I was grateful when she patted the seat next to her, since I feared gazing at Lisa would give our secret away. Mel eyed me up and down so blatantly that I blushed. The energy crackled between us, and had I not been devoted to Lisa and about to show off for the crowd, I wouldn't have been able to resist. Some women have that magic that lets them top you without saying a word. Mel possessed that trick in spades. So did Lisa, but I could tell that Mel would put me through my paces in a different way than my wife.

The hairs on my left arm stood up as I listened to Lisa explain the basis of BDSM. "And now we're going to watch how a scene happens. Does anyone want to be my demo bottom?"

Immediately, hands went up all across the room. I didn't want to look too eager, so I waited a few crucial seconds. I stuck my right hand in the air and felt Mel's stare get even more intense. Lisa looked around the room, gazing all the way to the back before easing forward, then settling in the middle. On me. "How about you?" she asked.

I must have looked somber as I stood up. "Me?" I asked meekly, lest I burst out laughing. Yet my body was vibrating with a tension that was all too serious.

"Yes, you. Bad Girl. Get up here."

Lisa smiled at the crowd, then beckoned me closer. "Kneel while I explain what's going to happen." I sank to my knees. She was my wife, but in that moment, she was someone else, someone even hotter than Lisa.

I knelt, though I felt only a little like myself in that moment. "Bow your head and kiss my shoes." I bent, the motion pulling my thong tight against my pussy—the thong Lisa had instructed me to wear.

"Very good. Now I'm going to show which parts of the body can be safely spanked. Take off all your clothes except your panties. If you're even wearing any." I couldn't help but blush at the tone in her voice, one that implied a girl like me wouldn't be wearing any panties. I scrambled out of my clothes and stood practically naked in front of a crowd of strangers, save for Mel, who was staring at me with unabashed lust.

"What's your name?"

"Dawn."

"Okay, Dawn. Have you ever done this before?"

"No," I answered honestly—I'd never been a demo bottom before.

"So you're a kinky virgin, but you think you're into pain, right?"

"A little," I said, trying not to giggle.

"What about submitting, being told what to do, that type of thing?"

I looked at her, my gaze boring into hers for a few beautiful seconds. "I'm pretty sure I'd be into that," I conceded.

"Very good, then. If there's anything you don't want me to do, use the safeword 'red' for stop." She turned to the crowd. "You can make up your own safeword, anything short and easy to remember, that wouldn't normally come up in the course of play. For you, Dawn," she continued, turning back to me, "the word 'yellow' will mean you like what I'm doing but want me to ease off a little. Some people play with a word like 'green' for go, but for our purposes, I'm going to decide how much pain I want to inflict on you, and you're going to take it." A sneering taunt had crept into her voice.

Then Lisa officially started her lesson, sweeping one hand from my head to my thigh. "Now, you already probably know about certain sensitive body parts, like the nipples," she started as she grabbed each of mine. "Feel free to tug, twist or smack the nipples," she said, demonstrating each action. "You can even bite them, but be careful about how intensely you do so. Me, I'm a big fan of nipple clamps. Like these."

"You okay with that, Dawn?" she asked, her voice giving nothing away. Lisa's cool, calm, professional manner made me wetter than I could remember being in ages. It was like taking a new lover, in a way—I felt like someone else, and she was this kinky teacher rather than the woman with whom I'd walked down the aisle.

"Yes," I said.

"That's 'yes, ma'am,' next time," she snapped. I didn't fake the shudder that went through me at her words.

If you think wearing nipple clamps is no big deal, you haven't had Lisa put them on you. She didn't just let the toys do the work; no, Lisa made sure both of my nipples were primed and ready. Painstakingly slowly, she gave the audience a view from the side of how she stretched my nubs, then flattened them, then tugged them between her teeth. She gave them quite the workout before they were allowed to be nestled snugly between the metal clamps.

"Now, class, where is it safe to use this riding crop?" she asked, showing off a black one studded with some sort of glittering crystals at the handle. She must have borrowed or purchased it, since I'd never seen it before.

Instead of raising their hands, the class called out answers in a cacophony of voices. I heard "ass," "inner thighs," "nipples," "underarms" and "the bottoms of her feet."

"You have been paying attention," Lisa praised the room. "You don't want to use the riding crop or a whip or flogger on anyone's face or head, or directly on knees, elbows or any sensitive areas. But you are more than welcome to do this"—she said as she brushed the tip of the toy against my cheek, then down to my lips. "Kiss it," she ordered; I instantly puckered up. Somehow, even the simplest command sounded so much hotter up here as "Dawn."

"I'm going to ask you a question, Dawn, and I want you to answer honestly. Have you ever had your pussy slapped?"

I couldn't help the moan that left my mouth.

"No, ma'am," I said. Thankfully I wasn't lying because she'd never actually done that. She'd cupped it, pinched my clit, and hit my inner thighs—but never there.

"Are you willing to try it in front of all these people?"

"Yes." The silence echoed through the room. "Ma'am."

"Then get down on your knees and beg me for it."

I dropped to the ground. "And show me that pussy first so I know exactly what you're asking for."

I scrambled to pull down my very wet panties. She bent to stare at me, then snapped her fingers and beckoned two obedient butch assistants with close-cropped hair to bring a table over that had been tucked in a corner. It was covered in white paper. "Get up here," Lisa barked.

I quickly did as directed, my back on the table. "Now spread your legs and show everyone what you just showed me. I'm going to have them be the judge of whether you should get your pussy smacked."

This was even more humiliating, but all the hotter for it. I spread my legs, but I didn't do a good enough job, because Lisa pushed my knees farther apart, then told the assistants to grab hold of my feet and hold me wide open. "So, kinksters, what do you think? Should Dawn get her pussy slapped with this riding crop?"

The room erupted in applause. I was glad they couldn't see me blush. I was shocked at how far Lisa was taking this—a good kind of shock, like a current of energy reigniting our relationship. Or rather, Dawn's and Lisa's.

"Well, I guess that answers the question. But since this is a class, I am going to give some hands-on lessons in how to strike such a delicate area. Who wants to try it?"

When I lifted my head for a moment, it seemed like half the room had formed a line to volunteer—and there was Mel, right at the front. This was mortifying—but also very, very hot. Usually, when I know a secret, I cling to the knowledge, feeling special for having insight others don't. This time, it felt more like the reverse, as if the crowd knew something about me that I didn't, as if I really were the kinky virgin I was pretending to be, but they could tell just how masochistic I was. I knew at least one thing for sure, though—Lisa was enjoying this as much as I was. She had a big grin on her face as she welcomed Mel to stand right before me.

They conferred in whispers, then Mel said, "Spread your legs wider." I did, pressing against the hands securing me.

"Too bad we don't have a cross or a spreader bar," Lisa muttered as someone else whistled.

Mel took the crop and ran it up my left inner thigh, bypassing the aching place between my legs in order to run it down the same path on my right inner thigh. Then she pressed it against my mons, up over my belly, detouring to one breast followed by the other, lifting my chin to meet her gaze. "Where do you want to be hit?" Was this reverse psychology, where she'd zoom straight to another part? I didn't let myself think too much before blurting, "My clit. My pussy."

The whap against my nipple startled me. "You sure you can take it, *virgin?*"

I stared right back into Mel's eyes. "Yes, I'm sure."

With Lisa offering guidance, Mel took the crop and tapped it against my clit. I trembled, wishing I were secured to a cross or spreader bar myself, because when she hit me again harder, I started to tremble, though the human restraints were working very well. My captors clearly took their job seriously. When the crop moved from my clit to my slit, I balled my fists at my sides, shutting my eyes and letting sensation take over. The taps became slaps, loud enough to almost drown out the crowd's murmurings. I wasn't prepared for another crop to join the mix, but soon each nipple *and* my pussy were being treated to delicious torment.

Lisa cut the demo short—or at least, it felt short, even though my pussy was throbbing and it felt good to be given the chance to put my panties back on and sit. I didn't get relief until I went back to my room and had an explosive orgasm, followed by another one while standing under the shower spray.

CRED

AFTER THAT FIRST TIME, I GOT REALLY INTO IT, AND STARTED RESEARCHING more places we could go and act out this roleplay. I started shopping for the woman I came to think of as a new woman each time. Sometimes she wore a wig or a temporary tattoo; she shopped not at custom corset or latex shops, but cheap off the rack type stores. She rarely wore panties. Sometimes she was bratty and sometimes she was obedient. Sometimes she was lucky and got to take a fist or a cock. Sometimes she got spanked with a firm hand; other times she was lucky enough to earn a paddle or whip. Always she loved having her mouth full.

The more I played the role, the less I was acting. I got into the idea of being a forty-three-year-old kinky virgin. Was that woman like me when I'd first stepped into a play party at nineteen? Or was she even hungrier for it, after learning about the way the real world worked? Either way, the moment when Lisa reached up and revealed that, yes, indeed, beneath that super tight dress I wasn't actually wearing any panties, I got a thrill like no other—not even like when we played alone. Becoming an anonymous submissive, masochistic slut who wanted nothing more than to show off in front of a crowd made me giddy, a rush of endorphins and exhibitionism filling my body each time.

Yesterday, knowing how bruised I was from our own play, Lisa surprised me yet again. Instead of making me (or rather "me") strip, she let me keep my slinky black dress on, though she did pull it down to do a quick demo on how to slap a woman's tits properly. Then she asked for volunteers who had the biggest cocks to come forward before "teaching" me how to deep-throat, and them how to face-fuck a very willing, hungry, horny participant. It didn't take long before I was able to fit even the biggest one all the way down my throat. "She's a quick study, isn't she?" Lisa patted me on the head.

"As a reward, we're going to try it again. But this time, I want you to pretend you don't want it. We're going to play out a rape fantasy. Anyone want to hold her down?" I'd already filled out a yes/no/maybe list—after Lisa explained what that was—indicating I was up for being "forced," but I hadn't actually expected her to go there. Still, this wasn't a beginner's class, but an advanced one; I was the exception. Lisa had made sure to grill me in front of everyone to make sure I knew what I was getting into. From the reaction she'd gotten, it was clear that even kinky dykes love fresh meat. One voluptuous woman wearing a velvet and lace dress came forward, along with some wiry but strong-looking bois. "Okay, you each grab a limb," said Lisa.

"You, girl—struggle hard." I shut my eyes and fully embraced the moment—I'd struggled and wrestled with Lisa, but it's different when it's the woman you love. These were strangers, and in that moment, one of them was prying my lips open.

"Give me that slutty little mouth," one said before slapping my face. I clamped my lips shut and turned my head left and right, until hands reached down and stilled it in place. I opened my eyes to see a fierce look on the face of the one with the biggest cock from earlier.

I knew I had to do my best now, because once the cock was in my mouth, no matter how good an actress I am, I'd want to suck it. I set my own face in a defiant tone and tried to kick my legs out from my assailants. They held tight, one clamping

nails into my ankle when I tried to fight back.

The butch straddling my chest bent down and bit the side of my neck. "Give me what I want, whore." I didn't wear down that easily. I listened to the pants and heavy breathing and heard Lisa narrating, even though I was too gone to recognize her exact words. I breathed through my nose, imagining breathing out fire. The cock slapped me across the cheek. "You're gonna get this nice and wet so I can shove it up your ass."

I finally had to take a breath through my mouth, and when I did, I was instantly greeted with silicone. I spat it back but it found its way into my mouth once again. When a hand made for my neck, resting there but implying greater pressure, I let the cock go deeper. I opened my eyes and shared a moment with the cock's owner before that became too much for me. Unbidden, tears rolled down my face as one hand massaged my neck while the cock eased in and out. I'm not sure how long it went on for but I was in a daze when I was finally released to a rousing round of applause. "I'll save your ass for next time," my partner sneered.

"Let's hear it for all of today's volunteers, but especially this one. I think she deserves a nice hot soak in the Jacuzzi." I smiled. Lisa knew that was my favorite way to relax.

CR80

AFTER I WAS SUFFICIENTLY WARM, THOUGH STILL SORE IN VARIOUS PLACES, Lisa and I dared to head back to her room together. "So...did you really like it?" she asked a bit shyly.

"Couldn't you tell?"

"Well, I thought so, but I wanted to be absolutely sure. Because I want to do that with you, too. Just us."

I pulled her on top of me, sank back against the pillows and kissed her hard, grateful that being a kinky virgin was only a once-in-a-while treat. With Lisa, I could be as perverted, filthy, slutty and masochistic as I wanted to be. Good thing, too, because we'd only scratched the surface.

TOO OLD FOR THIS
Giselle Renard

DID LARISSA STILL BELIEVE WHAT SHE'D SAID ALL THOSE YEARS AGO? Maybe she'd changed her mind since then. Hopefully she had...

"Let me see that pretty pussy."

Minnie's eyes nearly jumped out of their sockets. "Shhh! People will hear you."

Larissa cocked her head. "So shut the door."

There was so much work piled up on her desk—checks to cut and invoices to follow up on—but Minnie couldn't say no. When Larissa got that gleam in her eye, all those pressing office concerns snapped away like the crack of a whip. Anyway, it was Larissa's company. If the boss wanted the door closed, Minnie would just have to close the door.

"Turn down the blinds," Larissa said, her sharp canines gleaming. "Then park your ass on my desk. You know the drill."

"Yes, Boss." Minnie fumbled with the blinds. If she took too long, she might incur an unbearable punishment. "Sorry, Boss. The thing is sticky."

"*The thing?* Is it really?" Larissa pushed her chair back, closer to the window. No blinds on that one, and it ran carpet to ceiling. Even on the twenty-eighth floor, Minnie wondered if other office workers in other office towers diddled themselves as they watched her daily submission. Seemed unlikely, but maybe someone out there had a telescope?

Anyway, if anyone really was watching, their eyes would no doubt be glued to Larissa. Minnie felt like she'd aged twenty years in the past five, but her boss only grew more striking with age. At thirty-six, Minnie's auburn curls were dappled with gray while Larissa's straightened hair ran jet-black along her scalp, pulled tightly into a golden clip, long extensions cascading down her back. No wrinkles marring the dark skin under those blazing eyes.

Larissa could have been a supermodel. Hell, she still could be. If there were a pageant for business executives, she could strut across the stage in that sharp suit jacket and fearsome leather skirt. Crisp white shirt, jewels and gold. She'd take top prize.

Minnie swished around the office in her summer skirt before hopping on Larissa's desk. Ooh, was she ever wet! When had that happened? Seemed like every time Larissa gave her that hungry look, her pussy swelled, her clit throbbed, and hot juice spilled down her thighs.

"Open your legs, little miss."

Her throat ran dry, but she hiked her feet off the carpet and hooked her heels into the drawer handles. The veneer on Larissa's mid-century modern desk was scuffed in two spots, from Minnie's two feet: small black stripes from every pair of heels she'd ever worn.

"Wider." Larissa pointed back and forth between both knees. "Wide as you can."

"Yes, Boss." Minnie parted her thighs until her muscles screamed. "How's that?"

"It'll have to do," Larissa faux-clucked. "Now hike up your skirt."

Minnie took the diaphanous fabric between her fingers and thumbs, tossing it around to tease her boss. "Up?"

"All the way." A bit of a growl, now. "Up past your hips. Then unbutton your blouse and lean back."

Hiking up her wispy skirt, Minnie imagined what her boss must be seeing. She could tell by the hot gleam in Larissa's eyes when she'd lifted far enough. Larissa was the type to play her cards close to the chest, but Minnie could always tell when the wolf caught sight of its sweet prey.

"Good," Larissa said, almost a sneer. "No panties. Very nice."

"And the garters, Boss? Do you like the stockings and garters?"

Larissa's expression hardened. "Don't push your luck."

Ooh, Minnie had really gotten to her today! The garters were always a hit.

"Unbutton that blouse." Leaning forward, Larissa grabbed a letter opener from her desk. The weapon had a thick jade handle. Minnie had met it before. "Quick, or I'll slice those buttons off and you'll have to walk around all day with your top hanging open."

"You love making me blush, don't you, Boss?"

Minnie was really pushing her luck. She knew that. But if she got off on praise, she got off even more on admonitions.

"You'd like that," Larissa sneered. "Having to walk these halls with your bra showing, your tits hanging out. You like it when people stare. You want to be the center of attention."

"No, Boss. Not at all."

"Think you can fool me?" Tracing the letter opener around Minnie's top button, Larissa somehow managed to drive it into the hole and pop it off . The button went flying across the room, landing on Larissa's abandoned office chair.

"Oh no."

Larissa's expression darkened. "You love it."

"I'll do the rest." Minnie's fingers trembled as she slipped the next button through its hole. Not easy to undress on demand, even after all these years. She wanted to please Larissa, impress her. Strippers make it look so easy.

Her bra was white lace, and it captured Larissa's gaze even though she'd worn it many times before.

"You like?" Minnie asked, propping her breasts up with both hands. "If you look, you can just make out a hint of my nipples through the pattern. Can you see them?"

"Peachy," Larissa said, nodding. She traced the hazardous end of her letter opener down the curve of Minnie's breast, right near the border of lace.

"Cold." Minnie tried not to shiver. Goosebumps rose across her bare flesh as her boss' weapon teased her skin. "Feels good."

"Oh?" Larissa turned the letter opener forty-five degrees, digging the dull edge into her breast. "Is that better?"

The metal wasn't sharp. It jabbed Minnie in a way that made her crave more intense pain. She thrust her tits forward, driving them against the edge, watching her skin indent around the dull blade. Her boss refused to cut her with anything sharp. She'd asked before.

"Pull down the cups." Larissa traced the warming metal against the lace edge of her bra, drawing it away from her skin, but only slightly. "I want to see your tits."

She said it like she'd never seen them before...like she hadn't touched them, licked them, felt them, bitten them, every workday for the past five years. Like Minnie's body was new and exciting. Every day, when she exposed her breasts to her employer, it was new and exciting all over again. This never got old.

Larissa didn't often remove clothing, so Minnie's breath caught when she unbuttoned her tailored suit jacket. Without taking it off, she slipped open her top, like its buttons were magnets she only had to slide her fingers across to undo.

Her tits were small. She didn't wear a bra, didn't need one, especially when her jackets always covered up her chest. Her brown skin shone in the afternoon sun, which reflected off the business sector's many mirrored windows.

Minnie watched in unsanctioned awe as her boss' dark nipples puckered, hardened to sharp buds. She didn't know what to say when Larissa drew closer, pressing those pointed nipples to hers. Their tits touched, and a bolt of arousal traveled Minnie's body, swirling like a maelstrom in her belly. Larissa's erect nipples pressed into her softer skin, teasing her, taunting her, making her feverish.

"What are you craving?" Larissa asked.

Her pussy ached. She couldn't speak.

"Nothing?" Larissa's mouth was so close Minnie could feel her boss' breath in her ear. "You mean your pussy isn't wet for me? Your nipples don't want to be sucked?"

Minnie's throat ran dry. She tried to tell her boss how badly she wanted her pussy fucked, but no sound came out. Hot juice dripped from her cunt, down her ass crack, soaking her skirt. She'd have a wet spot there, just like every other day. There was a reason she bought skirts with busy floral patterns—so her co-workers wouldn't notice the splotches of nectar soaking through.

"What about this?" Larissa asked, holding the letter opener by its blade. "You want me to fuck you with it?"

Nodding, Minnie pushed a faint sound past her lips: "Please."

Why did she get so nervous? Every day? She should be used to this by now. It shouldn't be so enthralling, but every morning she dressed for a hot date and came into work with her heart battering her ribs. Though she was in and out all day, each time she set foot in her boss' office, her clit throbbed. Would this be the time Larissa made a pass at her? Asked her to close the door?

Minnie never took initiative. She always waited to be told what to do. At this point, it was like Larissa had a responsibility to her. Her employer paid biweekly, provided free coffee, and took care of her sexual needs. A sweet deal, but Minnie couldn't help worrying their arrangement would come to a screeching halt at any moment.

Dragging her hard nipples down Minnie's bare belly, Larissa said, "I can follow the smell of your cunt. It's especially strong today."

"Is it?" Minnie felt her cheeks light up. "I don't know why."

"Did you wash for me this morning?"

"Of course. I always do."

"Were you running around a lot?"

Minnie hesitated. Back and forth between the bank and the post office? Yes, she'd been on her feet all day.

"I can smell your sweat." Larissa snatched a wet wipe from her desk drawer and cleaned the thick jade handle of her letter opener. "Hot pussy and perspiration, you bad girl. You dirty girl. Are you trying to put me off?"

"No, Boss. I'm sorry."

Grabbing another wipe, Larissa rubbed it over Minnie's wet pussy. "I shouldn't have to do this—clean you like a baby. It's your responsibility to stay sweet for me."

"I know." Minnie's heartbeat thundered in her ears as Larissa tossed the wipes in the trash. "Tomorrow I'll smell sweet as pie."

"Good." Larissa circled the rounded jade around Minnie's slit, not quite pressing it in, not quite touching her clit. "How does that feel, hmm?"

Minnie swallowed hard. "Tickles."

"Tickles?"

"Teases." Her breath came on so fast her exposed breasts surged against her pulled-down bra. "It's not enough. I want more."

"More?" A wicked smirk crossed Larissa's painted lips.

"I want it inside me."

"Inside?"

"In my pussy." Leaning back on her elbows, Minnie cradled her breasts with both hands. "I want you to shove it up my snatch and fuck me with it."

"Push your tits together." Larissa's dark brown nipples seemed to harden as she spoke. "Roll the nipples between your fingers. That's right." She nudged Minnie's clit with the jade handle, just gently, not exerting nearly enough pressure. But she knew what she was doing. "Now raise those big breasts to your lips. Suck them."

Minnie's clit throbbed against the mint-green rock. She wrapped her mouth around one swollen nipple, and felt her tongue's velvet heat soaring from her breast all the way down to her sopping wet pussy.

"Your *breasts*." Larissa whacked Minnie's pussy lips, using the letter opener like a club. "Both of them. Both at once."

"Both?" Minnie's brain buzzed as jade spankings struck her mound. "Both my tits? In my mouth?"

"Yes," Larissa said. "Suck them both."

Holding her heavy breasts against her chin, Minnie bowed her head and opened her mouth. She squeezed her tits together until they met against her tongue, and then closed her lips around both nipples. She'd never done this before. It felt strange for a moment, trying to suckle two tits at once, but the second she found her groove, liquid pleasure travelled her veins, filling her body with swirling gushes of heat. Her skin tingled and her muscles trembled. She gazed beseechingly at her boss as she sucked both breasts.

Larissa slipped the letter opener between her slick pussy lips and entered her with the bulging knob of jade. Minnie's cunt had no memory, when it came to fucking. Every time felt like the first. Her slit was tight and reluctant, but her juice coated the makeshift cock as it forged a path between her thighs.

"How does it look?" Minnie wanted to ask, but she worried Larissa would be displeased if she stopped sucking her tits. She wished she had a better view as her boss filled her pussy with jade.

"I don't like this. Get down," Larissa instructed. "Both feet on the floor. Both tits on the desk."

Minnie whimpered because it felt so good, sucking both nipples. She didn't want to stop. But if that's what Larissa wanted...

"Like this?" she asked once she'd climbed down and inverted herself.

"Hands behind your back." Larissa tucked Minnie's summer skirt under her arms, and then yanked the waist of her garter belt over her wrists. "Can you escape?"

"I could if I wanted to," Minnie admitted. "But I don't want to."

Minnie could see her boss' expression in her mind's eye: impressed and satisfied. Then Larissa grabbed Minnie's hair and yanked it until her breasts rose off the desk. "What about now?"

"I still don't want to escape," Minnie said. "Really, I just want you to fuck me."

A long moment passed, and all Minnie could feel was her hair pulling sharply on her scalp. The blinding pain made her cringe, and her pussy tightened as the letter opener found it. Larissa chuckled as she forced the bulge of jade deeper into Minnie's cunt, like this was funny.

"Again," Minnie begged when her boss bottomed out. "Slow. And twist it."

Her breasts sat like heavy cushions against the desk, supporting her while she leaned back. The garter elastic cut into her wrists, but nothing hurt as much as she wanted it to. Not even the steady thumping of jade as it rammed her tight cunt.

Every so often, Larissa stopped fucking her, pausing with the handle inside Minnie's snatch. Her boss swirled the jade cock, moving it in roving circles, making it feel larger, like the hard rock was expanding her slit. The blade must be digging into Larissa's palm by now. She only wished it was digging into hers. Even without a cutting edge, that slicing pain would feel wonderful.

"I'm about to make you come," Larissa said.

With nothing but a letter opener? Minnie seriously doubted that, but she said nothing, just listened as her boss opened a desk drawer and fished around for something. She didn't get a chance to see it before she heard a buzz and Larissa pressed something smooth and relatively flat over her mound.

"Oh my god!" Minnie cried.

Larissa let go of the letter opener just long enough to smack her ass. "Quiet down. You want your co-workers to know what you're up to in here?"

"No, no, no..." The vibrating thing, whatever it was, pulled an orgasm out of her, easy as sucking a milkshake through a straw. She bit her lip and clamped down on the jade cock, but that only intensified her climax. She whimpered, struggling not to, but unable to keep the little whinnies inside.

"You want the whole office talking about you?" Larissa scolded. "They'll say you slept your way to success. They'll whisper dyke when you walk by. They'll joke about you licking the boss-lady's girly parts. Is that what you want, Minnie?"

Vibrations traveled her arms and legs like little bolts of lightning, finding her fingers and toes, making them dance with arousal. Larissa fucked her so hard it hurt and finally, finally, Minnie got a taste of the pain she craved.

"Oh god!" Minnie squealed. "Hurts. Feels so good."

Larissa slapped her ass. "Keep your voice down."

"No!" She'd never rebelled like this before, but her pleasure and pain mingled with fear of rejection. "I don't care who knows. You do! You care!"

She cringed, expecting Larissa to smack her ass silly, but not a single blow landed. She waited, but nothing. Her belly whirled and buzzed. Her thighs trembled. The vibrator between her thighs brought on wave after wave of orgasm, and she folded her face against her breasts to muffle the sound.

Larissa turned the jade knob like a corkscrew, withdrawing it slowly from Minnie's swollen cunt. She panted viciously, rising and falling as her breasts pressed firmly into the desk. Her boss was strangely silent, almost absent.

Tearing her tingling hands from the waist of her garter, she turned sharply to meet Larissa's vacant stare. "Did I do something? What's wrong?"

"What did you mean when you said that I care?" Larissa asked. "You think I'm ashamed of something?"

Minnie wasn't sure how to answer. Leaning back against the desk, she caught a glimpse of the vibrator in her boss' hand and wanted to ask about it—the toy was green and looked like a leaf— but now was not the time.

"You think I'm ashamed of *us*?"

Without meaning to, Minnie nodded. "Only because...well, don't you remember? When we first started this, you kept telling me it wasn't serious, you weren't a lesbian, we weren't a couple. You said we were getting too old for this, and if we were still at it when you turned forty you'd kill yourself."

Larissa's jaw dropped. She said nothing.

"You don't remember?"

She shook her head. "I was young. I was stupid."

"So when you had your birthday the other week, I thought..." Tears bit Minnie's hot throat. She tried not to cry. "I've just been waiting..."

"I'm so sorry." Larissa wrapped her long arms around Minnie, bringing their bare breasts together. "What a *stupid* thing to say."

"Then it isn't true?"

"Of course not." Her boss petted her hair, breathing warmly in her ear. "It wasn't easy for me, coming to terms with being kinky, being queer. I fought it for a long time, even after we started this. People look at me, even other lesbians, and they say, 'You must be straight. You're just messing around. You're just experimenting.' Nobody was there for me. Nobody but you."

Minnie hugged her hard, squeezing their bodies together until tears burst out. As Larissa offered sweet words of consolation, Minnie sobbed on her shoulder—tears of joy, tears of relief. She would never be too old to cry.

THE DAME

Styx St. John

SHE APPEARED RIGHT IN THE MIDDLE OF *NIGHT TRAIN*, MAKING AN ENTRANCE like a character from the pages of a pulp magazine; white flapper dress, long string of pearls, white silk, elbow-length gloves, glittering heels, the whole nine yards. Her pastel cloche hat covered, but could not hide the short golden-blonde locks, or the look of excitement in bright, puckish eyes. She was a breathtaking beauty, though I suspected her methods of breathtaking were revealed only to the most private of company.

I should have known she was trouble, watching from one of the tables around the opulently decorated dance hall. In reality, the place had a day-to-day occupation as a movie theatre and rentable party space. This event was a fundraiser for medical supplies for the local hospital, and drew a lot of attention. The fact that it was a 1920s "Mystery in the Speakeasy" party made it even more attractive. Parties like these can give adults a chance to let loose, dress to the nines and have fun, while still managing to be tax deductible.

I was sitting with a group of my friends, most of us regulars at the local dyke bar. We weren't as fancy as some of the partygoers, in tuxedos and ballroom dresses, but we embraced a more *classic* look; dress shirts and slacks, wool vests and suspenders, wing tips, Doc Martens, driving caps, top hats or fedoras; a roughand-tumble gang crashing a party for the wealthy folks.

I had the foresight to wear my black fedora tilted over one blue eye, rakishly, as I looked out at the dance floor, moments before spotting the pretty dame. She had an entourage of three thick-necked goons with her; strong enough to bend steel with their hands, but none of them engaged in conversation, as a proper date would. Dane, a buddy of mine, noticed my attention was elsewhere and spied the lady and her entourage. She gave a whistle, raising an eyebrow in appreciation.

"Hot damn, she's one fine Sheba," Dane grinned at me, nudging my ribs with her elbow as she used some of the *lingo* she had learned all but five minutes ago. "You gonna ask her to cut a rug?"

I gave a confident smirk, tilted my hat back and stared at Dane for a few seconds, as if to say, "Just watch me work." Raising my head confidently as I stood, my hands smoothed imaginary wrinkles out of my clothing, fingers pulling taut the folded cuff s of my sleeves, black vest silhouetting slight curves, gray tie pressed between the vest and the white button down shirt matched with black dress slacks and shoes; I looked sharp, and I knew it. Over the music I could barely hear the faint clicking of my shined shoes on the marble floor as I made my way toward her.

She looked up, moments before the bodyguards noticed me. That gave me a moment to appreciate her bright green eyes a bit longer than was necessarily polite. The light of the dance hall caused them to shine like twin emeralds. I stood on her left, smack-dab between two of the torpedoes. I had my hand out toward the dame an instant before one of the bears could growl at me.

"Cigarette?" I said casually, holding out the pack of candy cigarettes with one of the thin white sticks poking from the opening at the top. With the clean-air laws passed last year, we couldn't smoke in the theatre, but the organizers had purchased candy cigarettes and bubble-gum cigars for patrons to buy, along with pretty trinkets for the dolls.

She looked up at me, those sparkling eyes locking with mine, and I felt my heart rise up toward my throat. To my chagrin, she shook her head. "No, thank you, I don't smoke," she replied softly, her voice like smooth velvet. One of her guards made to grab my shoulder and guide me away. Just then her eyes lit up with impish glee. "But I wouldn't say no if you wanted to buy me a drink."

It took at least five seconds before my brain got the message. I nodded once, knowing my grin was much larger than it should have been.

After a trip to the bar, I returned with three waters for the entourage, a Southside for myself and a White Lady, Savoy style, for the dame. She took a sip, her dark red lips wrapped around the straw as her eyebrows rose in appreciation. "Thank you," she smiled at me, gesturing with a hand toward the empty chair beside her. "Won't you have a seat?"

Taking off my fedora, I gladly joined the party at the table. She introduced herself as Miss Charlotte, a patron of the arts who had attended parties like these since she was little. It turned out the three bruisers were friends of hers that she convinced to join the festivities this evening. I didn't realize how friendly they were until I noticed two of them holding hands underneath the table. One of the fellows caught my eye, gave me a brief wink, and then a mock snarl. I glanced away, but grinned and winked back.

"And what's your name?" She looked to me, one slim eyebrow raised. A low drumbeat echoed in the room, as I recognized the tune; the Beastie Boys' *Song for Junior*.

I took a sip of my drink, sighing. I grinned at Miss Charlotte, tipping an imaginary hat. "The name's Jack," I said. I'd made it up on the spot. "Worked my way up as spotter to the leader of the Broken Hearts Gang."

I had to give Miss Charlotte credit; she played along like a professional, her big emerald eyes widening in surprise. "Are you a... dangerous sort of person, Jack?" Her escorts caught that and all three glared at me with a glint in their eyes; staged or not, I had no doubt they'd give me the boot if I showed anything but the proper respect to their mistress.

I lowered my gaze, but not before giving Miss Charlotte a roguish smile. "Sometimes, Miss Charlotte, but never to a lady as proper and beautiful as yourself."

The lady smiled, laughing softly, and her three bodyguards relaxed just a little. I mentally wiped my brow, as that had been a shade too close for my comfort. Miss Charlotte made to push her chair back and before the others moved I was already out of my seat, pulling it out for her. She graced me with a courteous smile. "I'm going to the powder room...would you care to accompany me?"

I offered my arm, and her slim hand pressed on the sleeve of my shirt. Two of the guards stood, but she requested one wait and save the table for when we returned. Two of them followed us as far as the entry hall to the bathrooms and the coat check, where they stood and waited, backs to the wall like they were former military; who knows? Perhaps they were.

Walking with Miss Charlotte on my arm felt like anything but reality; I had noticed Dane's envious look, along with others from a few of our friends, as we walked past. If this really were a fantasy, we wouldn't be going to the bathroom...

"In here," Miss Charlotte said, pulling my arm suddenly toward the coat check. We were met by a tuxedoed man with glasses, obviously the man in charge of the coat room. Miss Charlotte didn't miss a beat as she slid a hand into her purse and pressed a folded-up Jackson into his palm. "I'll let you know when we're finished," she said. The clerk gave a curt nod, swiftly leaving us alone, surrounded by trench coats and expensive furs.

Before I could speak, she gripped the back of my vest and pulled me to her, our lips meeting in a hard, fierce kiss. My eyes closed as I lost myself temporarily, the scent of her perfume dizzying, more potent than my drink. I could feel her steady heartbeat against my body, my own thudding in my ears, the sound of her breath and mine loud and harsh in our close clinch. As we kissed, her hand slid from my back to my chest, and then lower, and lower still, until it gripped firmly; I gasped, leaning back and released her from our kiss. She smiled knowingly. "Why, Jack, is that a gun in your pocket or are you just glad to see me?"

I showed my teeth in a fierce grin, about to reach down to allow her better access; she slapped my hand away, her smile fading. I was about to say something, but it was lost as she leaned in again, hissing like a cat. "You don't get to touch, naughty boi. I want you to keep your hands behind your back, right now, or I leave you here with your fly undone and send my men in to take care of you."

I stared, incredulous, unbelieving...but stronger than any fear I felt was my desire for her. My hands moved back, gripping my forearms as I steadied myself, looking at her from under my fedora. The lady's smile returned, and she stepped in, holding me as she purred, whispering into my ear as she played with the tie at my neck. "That's a good boi.... I had a feeling about you, Jack, that you were just what I was looking for this evening."

My eyes closed from the heat of her words, my mouth opening in a warm sigh; she had me dead to rights and we both knew it. I wanted to speak, to say something, but I didn't know what, so I kept silent, listening to the lady's words.

"I want you to imagine all the things I could do to a tough like you," she caressed the back of my neck with sharp fingernails, goose bumps rising from the paths they took. "All the different ways I could tie you up and break you down to begging and pleading with me to give you my permission to come. Only I'll get off first and make you watch, just to drive you crazy with need. You'd like that, wouldn't you, Jack?"

I swallowed hard, my mind spinning with all the different imaginings running through it. Even if this was just a come-on, it was the best one I'd ever had. Licking my dry lips, I dredged up my almost-forgotten voice. "I like the way you think, Miss Charlotte."

The lady smiled and I was rewarded with another kiss, this one ablaze with raw desire. Her hand gripped my crotch again, this time sliding up and down, past the waistband of my slacks and my underwear. Her hand found where the strap-on ended and my body began, a finger sliding to press against and circle my clit. I moaned into her mouth, leaning forward to press closer as my hands were still behind my back. Her free hand gripped my shoulder and she guided me down to lie on the floor, slacks tight against my cock, arms positioned against the small of my back. She unzipped my pants and pulled down my underwear to reveal what I was packing. It was about six inches long, thick, veined and bright red. She looked at me: hat knocked off , my shirt in disarray, pants open to reveal a rather vulgar toy...I must've looked a sight.

Miss Charlotte raised an eyebrow, a silent question in her eyes. I nodded toward my left pocket. "Condoms," I said hoarsely, biting my lower lip. She reached in and pulled out a small purple square. Soon it was unwrapped and my cock was covered.

She raised her skirt, showing a fl ash of creamy white thigh and two pert, smooth lips between her legs; my chest rose and fell from the exertion, trying to keep from grabbing her and slamming into her as hard as I could. But etiquette dictated that it was the lady's prerogative.

I watched as she positioned the dildo at her slit, giving a faint moan as she slid down slowly, adjusting to the firmness now pressing inside of her. She continued slowly, so slowly, until her ass was resting on my thighs, the cock now firmly seated. I pressed my hips up slowly, teasingly, and she gasped, her surprised look replaced quickly by a warning glare. I felt sweat trickle down my face, nerves on edge and desire rushing through my blood, but I smiled all the same, giving a small nod. I understood; it was her ride.

And ride she did, slowly at first, leaning forward slightly and letting her hands rest on my chest. I could feel her fingers gripping through my clothes and onto my breasts and winced from the pain, but moaned encouragingly as she slid her fingers down, teasing and pinching at my now erect nipples.

My hands were numb from the white-knuckled grip I was giving my forearms. As she gained rhythm, bouncing up and down, controlling her movement with her legs, I couldn't take it anymore and I thrust my hips upward, meeting her downward movements. She nodded at me, panting, her whole body seeming to shine with the exertion. I had never seen anything more beautiful.

Eventually, I felt her legs shaking. She gripped my cock and pulled up just as she came—silently, without even a whimper. By this time I was so turned on. My nipples were hard and my clit ached to be touched. I looked up at her, my eyes wide, pleading, one word escaping my lips in a whisper. "Please..."

It was enough. With the toy inside of her, one hand found my clit, two fingers caressing the now slick, sensitive skin, the other hand sliding under my shirt and bra, switching from one breast to the other, pulling, gripping, pinching and clawing at soft breasts and hard nipples. I tossed my head back, moaning so loud I feared someone might hear, but I didn't care. My toes curled in my shoes as my hips rose and fell, pressing into the lady as I strained for release. My eyes were fixed on her face; I saw her tongue flicker out to lick at her lips as she smiled. "Come for me, boi..."

I went still for a second; then my body jerked, over and over, as the orgasm crashed hard through me, spreading outward until I collapsed, head turned to the side, panting for breath. My clothes were soaked, as if I had run a marathon. It certainly felt as if I had.

Miss Charlotte moved off me, unrolling the condom and placing it into the wrapping, which she folded up and placed in her purse. "A little reminder," she smiled.

She positioned the toy back between my legs, pulling my underwear and slacks up, zipping and buttoning them, even tucking my shirt in and straightening my vest. I was mystified, but continued to keep my hands behind my back, as she'd ordered. Emerald eyes smiled down at me. "I am sorry about this, Jack."

SNAP. I felt something cold against my chest and looked down; a red, spreading stain appeared on my shirt. My breath caught, until I noticed the fake blood capsule in her open palm. She leaned in, careful not to get the red on her dress. "One of the committee members asked me to find someone to play the victim in tonight's murder mystery, and I left it until too late.... You were too convenient to pass up."

I smiled, despite the situation.

"I knew a dame would be the death of me," I said, looking up at the lady. Even though the shirt was a favorite, I didn't care about it. Besides, it would be a heck of a memento.

Her hand slid to mine, still gripping my arms; she undid my tie, then wrapped it around my wrists, giving the appearance that I had been captured, and killed, which was the truth, of course. "Now when they find you, you won't be able to talk or tell who did this. So I'm trusting you to play along." Her emerald eyes glinted menacingly. I winked up at her, giving my assurance that I would not betray her trust. She smiled and pulled a handkerchief from her purse. She cleaned the lipstick from my face and rather than leave a new tell-tale smear, she blew me a kiss. Before she left, my hat was replaced, over my face. I had to admit, the lady was as thorough as a police detective; it made me wonder what her true occupation was.

I was left alone for about fifteen minutes, until I heard a scuffle and a cry of "Murder! Someone's been murdered in the coat room!" Eventually the hat was removed and I stared up into the faces of the crowd of party-goers, each one trying to figure out *whodunnit*.

Dane made her way in, once the majority of people left to give the costumed police their suspect's names.

"Can I say good-bye privately? She was a friend of mine," Dane asked the guard. He let her in and she knelt down next to me, shaking her head but grinning. "You son of a bitch, you got lucky, didn't you?" I just lay there, unable to hide my grin. My friend nodded. "I thought so. I'm supposed to give you this. The lady you were with asked me to, if you didn't talk." she held a card before my eyes. *Charlotte Hanover, Attorney At Law.* On the back was a hand-written phone number. She placed the card in my shirt pocket. I gave a small nod and a grin to Dane, who smirked back.

The party soon ended, with one of the wealthy socialites being tagged as the murderer. Miss Charlotte was cleared, as she had three solid alibis from her guards, and Dane obligingly kept her mouth shut, for which I owed her a twelve-pack of her favorite brew.

And as for me? I ended up calling Miss Charlotte for a date. We've been going out for five years now. And, every time I hear *Night Train*, or another classic jazz song, I smile to myself, thinking of the night Jack died. But what a wonderful death it was.... Oh, and I did keep my shirt.

TRIPTYCH

Lula Lisbon

"Beg me," I say, looking down at her. My voice is icy, and as I stare into her face I feel like a lioness toying with a bird. A very willing bird, with a penchant for being bitten. Her close-cropped, dark blonde hair is tousled, her wide eyes as stormy a gray-blue as a winter sea. Circling her, my stilettos clicking authoritatively on the hardwood floor, I note the glowing fuchsia ribbons that stripe across the pale skin of her back like a fancy gift-wrapped box. It pleases me. She is a present for myself that I've fastidiously decorated with carefully-placed lashes from my leather belt. It gives the impression that there are still layers and layers to be opened, to be unwrapped slowly— intimate secrets that even a nude body can still hide. I want to peel it all away, everything, to leave her so exposed for me that nothing else is left. Only she, and me.

I stop in front of her, reaching down with studied deliberation to adjust my stockings. I know my tight little skirt is riding up, flashing her a bit of black garter. I feel her eyes on me, ravenous. My nipples tingle, hyper-aware of the sheerness of the silk lace bra cradling the full mounds of my breasts.

"Please," she says. I hear a tinge of desperation in her voice. She doesn't talk much during our play, but due to her disobedience to me in this before, she's been on orgasm denial for three weeks to the day. I know she must be nearly out of her skin by now. My eyes flicker down to her mouth and catch the rapid movement of her pink tongue, darting out to wet dry lips.

"You know the deal," I tell her. "I will have total control of your body. You will tell me what you want, when I tell you. I want you trained to come with just my touch, with just my command. Has three weeks been enough, slaveboi? Or do we have to start over from the beginning?"

I relish the look of near-anguish that crosses her face, its appearance a dead giveaway of her complete submission. A low moan, soft yet guttural, rumbles in her throat. I lean forward, bending over her so that my long, strawberry-gold tresses trail against the smooth skin of her strong, bare shoulders. She shivers when I grab her by the nape of her neck and force her face upwards. With my other hand, I hike up my skirt to reveal the cock I've got strapped on underneath; hungrily, she opens to receive me.

Every day, she services me with her mouth as part of her training. Sometimes it's my cock, sometimes it's my cunt, and sometimes my ass—but always at my discretion. My little slut had never sucked a cock before mine, pristine gold star that she is, but I've rectified that. I enjoy looking down, holding her head, forcing my cock just a little deeper into her wet throat with every thrust. I can feel the base of it grinding against my clit, but I hold off for now. I want to see if her training has paid off , or if we'll have to start all over again. I'm patient, but not *that* patient. Either way, I have a plan.

I hook a finger through the ring in her collar and lead her to the bed. The duvet and sheets are embroidered aubergine Egyptian sateen, and her pale skin nearly glows like moonlight against the rich, nocturnal hue.

"Up," I command. She lies face-down at first, but I push her over onto her back, her ass at the edge of the mattress. All she's wearing is my collar and her butt-plug, the two things that have been established in our rules as mandatory at all times except with my express permission.

I love the subversive contrast of her masculinity and her submission to me, and accordingly, her accouterments are not feminine. The collar is sleek, studded and tough looking, and the plug is simple, utilitarian. In contrast, my lingerie is lacy and ultrafeminine, my spike heels impossibly high. I love my silky curves against the sharper angles of her body, and I love my total control over her. I let my oxblood-lacquered fingernails rake against her bare skin—hard then soft, soft then hard, enjoying the shades of crimson and rouge and rose that my touch brings up almost instantly. Her tits are small and creamy, her hips slim and her shoulders squarish, but her mound is softly rounded and lightly haired in dark blonde. Her nipples are larger and darker than one might expect, and my mouth waters to look at them. Her body is prey, and I'm hungry.

It's been far longer than I prefer since I've tasted her sweet cunt, but to indulge would have undermined her training and my own meted punishments, and so I've held myself back. Now, I want to see how quickly she can give in. Sinking to my knees between her thighs, I hold her wrists down as I attack her cunt with my tongue. The slickness of her juices slides against my cheeks where it has already coated the tops of her thighs. I dig my fingernails hard into her skin when she starts to writhe; it is both a warning and a command. After holding herself back for so long, maybe she's had herself trained to edge just a little too well, and I think perhaps she needs a bit of encouragement. My ruthless tongue zigzags across her cunt, plunges into her impossibly tight slit, traces the body-warm edge of the steel butt-plug before returning to the vanguard at her clit.

Her breath is ragged gasps; she hardly ever speaks when I fuck her, but I can tell where she is by her breath and by the pitch of her moans. I dig oxblood nails into the tender white flesh of her wrists again, and she obeys me. She stiffens, and a sweet legato note of passionate acquiescence escapes her. Her clit is hard, so hard in my mouth, and a sudden hot splash against my left cheek tells me she's squirted. I drink her in, delighting in how smooth and wet she is, how deliciously obedient. Finally, I slide up her nude body to invade her mouth. She laps her juices from my chin, my cheeks, and I guide her wrists together, up above her head, so I can hold them with my left hand as I position my cock with my right.

Without warning, I thrust up into her. I don't often fuck her cunt, preferring to save it as a delicacy for us both; but as tight as she is, there is nearly no resistance as she receives me. Once I'm past it, the bulge of her butt-plug only seems to pull my cock deeper into her, to keep me more securely inside her. Her knees tuck up, the soles of her bare feet positioning themselves at the backs of my thighs right underneath my ass cheeks. I twist my hips, dancing in her, working her g-spot as her little gasps drive me on like a whip. Her legs seem to draw me in and in and in, begging me in lieu of verbal pleas. I nip at her neck with my teeth, at the tender hollow of her clavicle, at the hardness of her creased deltoid. Her smell is intoxicating: cologne, sweat, and pussy, tinged with a sweet acridity I like to imagine is her pain. I take her nipple between my right thumb and forefinger, pinching hard at the zenith of a thrust into her.

"Now," I say, "now, pet, now!" and she writhes in response. I feel her falling into orgasm again, and I want to follow her, to plunge in after, but I am not done. While she is still gasping, overcome by the throes of passion three weeks postponed, I let go of her wrists. I slide out of her, and delicately, hesitantly, her arms drift down the deep, plummy expanse of the bed like a dancer's interpretation of falling snow.

My cock is slick and wet, resting against her mound, and I take a long moment to kiss her. I start off softly, delighting in the little shivers my kisses evoke in her. As the kiss deepens I alternate between rough and gentle, using lips and teeth and tongue, the contrast enflaming us both. We feed off each others' energy—her excitement heightens mine, and mine heightens hers in turn. I feel as if I'm drunk on her, drunk on her submission and pain, drunk on her lust and on mine. I hardly know where one stops and the other begins.

When I tuck the underside of her right knee into the vee of my left thumb and palm, forcing her leg up against her chest, she knows what I want next. I reach underneath her with the other hand and remove her plug, freeing her ass to let me in. She jumps when it suddenly pops out of her, her eyes gone wide and her breath shallow. She's pinned down by my gaze, helpless to do anything but look up at me. I watch her face carefully as I slide one finger down her slit, gathering up some of her moisture and circling the delicate pucker of her asshole before entering her. Her eyelids flutter, but she keeps her gaze locked on mine. She knows what I'll do if she breaks contact now.

A second finger joins the first, and involuntarily, she makes tiny little nods as I slide in. Her high-pitched moans drive me wild; the juxtaposition of such a pretty, girlish sound from my strong slaveboi is almost unearthly, almost profane how it excites me. A third digit, and she is stretched ever so tightly around me. Conversely, the more I fill her, the less she moves, as if by filling her up I'm also binding her down. She is tight, so tight, and I move my hand slightly inside her. My clit throbs against the base of my cock, and I know once I get there, I won't last long inside her. I sit up, my cock jiggling as I adjust my position. "Suck it, and suck it good, because it's all the lube you're getting." She nearly inhales it then, suddenly ferocious in her need for me. Jerking it with one hand, she makes it grind against my clit. The way her gray-blue eyes never leave mine as she swallows my cock whole makes my entire being ache for her—body, mind, soul. A trickle of saliva dribbles from the corner of her mouth, and with my free hand I wipe it from her face and lick it from my thumb. Inside her, I wriggle my fingers, and she shudders.

"Beg me," I say. "Tell me what you want." She suckles me for another long moment, then with hesitation lets my cock slowly go to emerge with a wet pop from between her reddened lips. Again, I swipe my thumb across her lip and suck it clean; I taste her pussy, her mouth, and her submission. She blushes bright pink. She is always shy about speaking, but she knows that telling me is part of her training, and she knows what will happen if I am not satisfied.

"Please," she says. "I want—I need your cock. I want—please, fuck my ass." Her voice grows louder in a rush then, in a fierce, fervent crescendo. "Use me, use my ass. I'm your slaveboi, I'm yours, only yours, and I want you to fuck me hard!"

I grin then, and she must see the predator in my eyes because I see a sudden glint of fear. It's like throwing a cigarette in a gas tank, and I almost come right then to see her look at me like that. I get between her legs and she pulls them up, putting her hands under her knees like she's been taught, holding her thighs tight to her chest. I pull out of her, adjust my cock, and give her my fingers to suck.

"Lick me clean, then, if you want me to fuck you hard." Reluctantly she opens her mouth, and as she sucks them in between her lips I plunge into her ass. Her eyes roll up into her skull, almost full white, as white as her skin, and she growls in helplessness. I don't hold back then, can't, won't—I pound her ass hard, fingering her mouth in tempo, claiming her body as my property. With every thrust comes another high-pitched moan, my favorite song from my favorite little bird.

"Do it, then, come on, do it!" I demand, fucking her harder. I feel myself edging, and I want to her to come with me. "Come now for me! Come with me!" There is no hesitation as she comes for me, and my clit throbs and pulses and I feel as if it is my real cock deep inside her ass, my hot living flesh inside hers. In the dreamy mindlessness of my climax I feel that we are one creature, at once both predator, both prey, both lost in one another, both falling and both plunging. Both flying, both feeding. Both fighting,

both fucking.

She is mine, and I am hers, and together we thrive. She is my slave, but in truth, she is the one who owns me—body, mind, soul.

ANGEL ON FIRE

Jessica Lennox

I CAN'T BELIEVE I'M ACTUALLY GETTING AROUSED, I THOUGHT, MY SKIN WARMING from the stinging blow to my ass. As the next blow landed, I recounted the events of the evening. My friend Adrian and I had been invited to a private dungeon for a play party, as had several of our friends. Adrian had a number of play partners in the community, and would surely be in some form of bondage by evening's end. I, however, had broken up with my partner/Master/Daddy four months prior, and was feeling pouty and irritable. I voiced my dismay to Adrian, who in turn suggested that I find a nice Mistress/Mommy to play with. I gasped with the horror of it, my eyes widening at the mere suggestion.

"Why not?" Adrian laughed.

"Because! I-I...no!" I stuttered.

"Oh come on. You might like it," Adrian suggested, with a wicked smile to punctuate the idea.

I sat there with a horrified look on my face, my brain struggling to wrap itself around the idea of playing with someone outside of my normal sandbox. "I wouldn't know what to do," I said, sounding rather pathetic.

"What do you mean?!" Adrian laughed, looking at me as if I had lost my mind.

"I don't know," I said plainly. "The thought of it makes me feel like I don't know which way is up! I know it sounds silly, but I'm so used to appealing to the masculine end of the gender spectrum, I'm not sure how I would appeal to someone like me. I mean, like me as in feminine," I explained.

Adrian gave me that 'are you serious?' look, then said, "I know what you meant, silly. Just be yourself. If the chemistry is there, it's there. In fact, I think I know the perfect person to introduce you to.

Her name is Evelyn Fire. I call her Ev, but if things go right, you'll be calling her 'Mistress Fire' by the end of the night." I frowned at the idea, and Adrian laughed. "She's moving to Baltimore in a couple of weeks, so this is a great opportunity to meet her, and if you don't like her, you never have to see her again." After a pause Adrian said, "I never told you this, but she asked about you once before."

"What?!" I exclaimed. "In what way?! I mean, what did she ask about me?!" Suddenly my ego was very curious, despite the fact that I hadn't been interested just seconds ago.

"She saw you at the Halloween party last year and asked who you were," Adrian continued. "I told her that you were my best friend, but that you were collared, and she said 'bummer' and that was that. I didn't tell you because I didn't see the point. I knew you wouldn't be interested anyway. But now, you're free—no collar—and it's time to shake off that moodiness and have some fun! Come on, what are you afraid of?"

I had to admit, I was slightly intrigued. But I'm not going to lie—I was probably more intrigued about her interest in me more than anything else. Regardless, I contemplated Adrian's question. What was I afraid of? Honestly, I was afraid my feminine wiles wouldn't work on a femme domme, and if that were true, how the hell was I going to manipulate the scene? Yes, I'm one of those pain-in-the-ass bottoms who basically tops from the bottom. I can manipulate the biggest, baddest butch daddy but I was pretty sure a strong femme domme wouldn't put up with that crap, so, how would that work? I started to feel a power struggle coming on already. If I wasn't willing to let go of that control, then it wouldn't work, right?

Wrong, my brain answered as it acknowledged another stinging smack to my right cheek and brought me back to the present. Okay, so back to how I got here.... Adrian convinced me, after much coercing, to at least an introduction. With me in tow, Adrian slowly weaved us through the various play spaces of the dungeon, peeking into every corner and alcove, looking for Evelyn. Part of me was secretly hoping she had left or was otherwise occupied, but no, just as I thought (with some relief) that we might not find her, Adrian exclaimed, "Ev! Come and meet my friend, Angel." I suddenly felt a knot in my stomach.

"Ah, yes, the lovely Angel," she said in a voice that was liquid velvet as she approached us. I wrung my hands nervously as I watched her. I *had* seen her before—who could forget that gorgeous hair, and everything else about her? I watched her play once and was surprised how absorbed I became. Evelyn was beautiful in a natural, but striking way. No makeup at all, as far as I could tell, but with that creamy skin and those dark, long lashes and beautiful, full red lips, you'd swear otherwise. Her dark, lush hair fell in natural waves down her back and over her shoulders, almost too gorgeous to be real. She had one of those curvy, luscious bodies, and made the very best of every feature by choosing the perfect complement of clothes to accentuate everything sexy about her. Her demeanor was so commanding that it was at once both intimidating and alluring.

She greeted Adrian warmly with a hug and a kiss, then reached out her hand to me, palm up. I unclasped my wringing hands and laid one of them upon hers, then watched with curiosity as she brought my hand to her lips. She held it there, pressing her lips very softly to my skin until I started to feel an internal conflict building—I wasn't sure if I liked it or not, and I fought the urge to pull my hand away. She must have sensed this because she said, "Relax, Angel, I won't bite unless you want me to." Then she released my hand slowly.

I didn't know what to say, so I didn't say anything at all. It was an awkward moment, and then Adrian suddenly chimed in. "Well, I see Jimmy over there, so I'll leave you two to get acquainted," and left me standing there, completely mortified, alone with Evelyn. I made a mental note to kick Adrian's ass later.

I forced a smile at Evelyn, and she said, "I don't mean to be forward, Angel, but it's getting late, so I'll cut right to the chase. Would you like a spanking? I'm very good at giving them."

I think my mouth actually dropped open, but frankly, I can't remember because I was so shocked that she had asked outright like that, so suddenly. I know several seconds must have ticked by as my brain reeled. Did I want one or not? Okay, this was ridiculous— when did I *not* want a spanking? Since we hadn't negotiated anything, I asked in response, "Would I have to get naked? And what instruments would you be using?"

"No," she answered, an endearing smile on her face. "I can simply lift your skirt up over your hips if that's comfortable for you. I'll be using nothing but my hand," she said, holding it up for me to see it.

I swallowed hard, then said, "Okay," in a nervous voice as I looked around for Adrian, or for any of my friends. Never one to miss an opportunity, Adrian was being cuffed to a padded wall, holding a candle in each hand and preparing to be flogged by someone I'd seen before but had never met. The rest of my friends were out of sight, probably engaged in similar scenarios of their own.

"Would you like to check in with someone first, Angel?" Evelyn asked, apparently sensing my uneasiness.

"No, thank you, I'm fine," I answered, even though the butterflies in my stomach felt like bats.

"Very well, let's get started, then," she said, motioning me over to a small padded stool. "Go ahead and lean over this. Get as comfortable as you can. What's your safeword?"

"Red," I answered.

"Red. Got it." She waited a few seconds then said, "Are you ready?"

"Yes," I whispered, leaning over and clutching the legs of the stool with my hands. Why was I so nervous? This certainly wasn't my first time being spanked, nor playing in public. *No, but this is your first time playing with another femme*, my inner voice reminded me, causing the bats to fl utter again. I silently told it to shut up as I tried to concentrate on what Evelyn was doing.

I felt her fingertips on my skin as she slowly traced the hem of my skirt, pulling it ever so slowly upward, eventually settling the fabric around my waist so it wouldn't be in her way. I shivered, unable to keep goose bumps from forming all over my skin.

"Relax, Angel," she said, her voice soothing and comforting.

I didn't think that was possible, but I took a deep breath anyway and unclenched my hands, willing my entire body to relax. "What should I call you?" I murmured, keeping my eyes closed.

"Mistress will suffice," she answered. For a moment, Adrian's smartass comment from earlier circled my brain, but left as soon as I felt Evelyn's hands on my skin. Her touch was soft and arousing, but I knew that wouldn't last long. Things were just getting started—foreplay, in a sense. I was desperately trying to get out of my own head and just enjoy it, but my inner bitch kept exclaiming "but she's a *femme!*" I silently screamed back "shut the fuck up!" as I felt her tracing patterns in circles on each of my buttocks, down my thighs, then back up again. I was beginning to feel aroused, and I let myself relax and think of all the elements about this that played into my arousal—playing in a public space, knowing others were watching, the anticipation of being spanked and feeling that delicious humiliation that comes along with it. I willed myself to absorb the moment, to indulge in all of those elements and give in to how wonderful her hands felt on my skin. I got so lost in it all that it took me awhile to realize that so far it felt like a happy-ending massage instead of the warm up for a spanking. What the hell? This wasn't what I had signed up for, or had I? No, of course not, I had seen her play before. It wasn't all feathers and rainbows—she had left some wicked marks on that sub. Maybe I had misunderstood her offer. Just as my brain started with another onslaught of questions, I felt the first stinging blow to the middle of my right cheek. I jumped from the unexpectedness, which was ironic, since this is exactly what I had been anticipating, and had agreed to. Then I felt another stinging blow, this time to the left side. Then another. And another. In between every few blows, she caressed my skin. I shivered, the contrast between those soft caresses and stinging blows were a delicious contradiction. That's when the *"I can't believe I'm actually getting aroused"* dialogue started. I felt my skin getting warm, but I wasn't sure if it was arousal from her caresses, or the sting from her smacks.

She delivered a particularly hard blow close to the inside of my thigh and I moaned, adjusting my feet slightly so that my legs were spread apart a little further. I know—naughty girl—but I couldn't help myself. I heard her make a noise, a loan moan in her throat. She began administering blows to different parts of my ass and thighs, a few of them so dangerously close to my pussy, she would have felt wetness there had she let her fingers move just another inch or so. Soon thereafter, the thought of having her hand touch my pussy became my entire focus. I silently pleaded and begged for her to let her hand slip just once, just a little. Whether she knew this or not, she kept her blows just above or to the right or left of where I really wanted her to go. It was maddening! I had no doubt she knew exactly where she wanted to hit me, and never missed her mark. I whimpered. I wiggled. I spread my legs even farther apart. Then the blows stopped all together. I was certain I had crossed a line, my sassy ways unwelcomed and utterly unappreciated. A few seconds passed. I didn't dare look up. Then I felt her directly behind me, pressing up against me.

"Is this what you want?" she asked as she reached down between my legs and stroked the very edge of my pussy.

I moaned as my knees buckled slightly. "Yes, please," I whispered.

"Yes, what?" she prompted.

"Yes, Mistress," I responded.

"Good girl," she said as she began massaging my pussy with the palm of her hand. She massaged it with the lightest touch, just like earlier with her caresses on my skin. It felt so good, but I wanted so much more. I tried to grind against her hand, but she wouldn't let me make any firmer contact. I whimpered, hoping she'd take pity of me, but obviously my feminine wiles weren't working on her—exactly as I had feared. She stepped back and landed a stinging blow to my left cheek, then traced her fingertips over the skin she had just reddened, then down and underneath to caress my pussy. I squirmed, trying to rub up against her hand, but she moved her fingers and dealt another stinging blow to my right cheek. I gasped, the pain competing with the pleasure I was feeling. Then she just started wailing blows nonstop, sometimes squarely to the middle of my ass cheeks, sometimes closer to the inside of my thighs, sometimes near my pussy where just the edges of her fingertips managed to make contact. She landed one softer blow directly to my pussy and I thought I was going to come. Now I was really squirming, the simultaneous stings from the spanking, and the intense arousal—also technically from the spanking, but probably more directly related to my intense need for her to touch my pussy. I gripped the legs of the stool and rocked back and forth on my heels as she continued to deliver perhaps the best spanking I'd ever had in my life. I was so close to coming, I clenched every muscle in my body and held my breath in anticipation. But then suddenly, she stopped. Completely. I let out a cry of despair and turned my head to look at her. She smiled at me warmly and said, "We're done for now, Angel. If you want to continue, come and see me in Baltimore in a couple of weeks. You were lovely." And with that, she walked toward the exit, leaving me standing there, bent over the stool.

I stayed there, bent over, with a look of disbelief on my face. Then a flash of anger ripped through me like lightning. I immediately stood up and smoothed down my skirt, making my way toward the bathroom. I chose the furthest stall from the door, locked myself inside it, and masturbated furiously until I felt that impending orgasm starting, the one I had so desperately wanted her to give me. My ass was on fire from the spanking, but my pussy was on fire from the entire experience. I pressed three fingers of my right hand fl at against my clit and rubbed as hard and fast as I could, while my left hand pinched one nipple through my blouse. I pictured Mistress

Evelyn's face as I rubbed and pinched myself, recalling how good her hands had felt on me, how wet and wanting she had made me. I couldn't hold back any longer. I took a deep breath and held it in, gritting my teeth as I felt my pussy clamp down and convulse over and over for what seemed like an eternity, finally leaving me spent. I leaned against the stall and gave myself a few minutes to catch my breath.

I exited the stall, grateful that nobody else was in the bathroom. As I washed my hands, I looked in the mirror and saw pure ecstasy on my face, and wondered how many miles it was to Baltimore.

MARES IN HEAT
Evey Brett

Sweat trickled down my back and between my breasts as I stood up to survey the day's work. I had to admit I was pleased. Tack room swept, organized and dusted, a pile of saddle blankets washed and dried and two dozen saddles along with their respective bridles polished and shined before the regional show tomorrow. All in all, it was a job well done, and I doubted even my bitch of a boss, Paloma, could find fault with it—though that was if she even deigned to notice my efforts at all.

One set of tack was still missing. Paloma had gone out into the sweltering Tucson night for one last practice ride, which meant that I couldn't go home until her mare was in and her tack was clean. I wouldn't have minded so much if I knew I'd at least get a *thank you*, but after having been the barn manager at White Dove Ranch for over three months I'd learned better.

I punched a saddle in frustration. "Ungrateful bitch," I muttered. Behind me, Paloma cleared her throat.

Shit.

Heart pounding, I turned around. There she was, riding whip in one hand and reins in the other. Her Lipizzan mare, Lucyna, curled her head around the tack room door and stared at me. Looking at Paloma, it was hard to tell she'd been riding. Her clothes, tan riding breeches which hugged her legs and ass along with the white button-up shirt showed no sign of dust. Neither did the shiny black boots which embraced her calves. Not a hair of her tight bun was out of place and her gloved hands were pristine.

My gut twisted, and it wasn't entirely from annoyance.

"There you are, Annie," she said in a bored voice. "See that Lucyna is properly taken care of." She dropped the reins in my hand and walked away.

I didn't know which made me angrier, that Paloma acknowledged my existence only as her servant, or the intimation that I would do anything other than properly care for any of her horses, especially her favorite Lipizzan mare.

Lucyna snorted and pawed the ground, her sign of impatience.

"Let's go," I told her. I led her to her stall where I exchanged her bridle for her leather halter. I uncinched the saddle and hung it on the rack along with her saddle blanket, which was damp and musky. Lucyna licked and chewed, obviously happy after her ride. I brushed and curried her round, muscular body, recalling the times I'd seen Paloma astride. They were perfectly matched, each moving in reaction to the other's body, a dance without words.

Like sex.

Shaking my head to clear it, I tucked Lucyna in before I got all hot and tingly thinking about things I shouldn't. It was an open secret at the barn that Paloma's lovers were all female. Rumor had it that she was as strict in the bedroom as she was in the arena, a dominant, and quite good at giving out what her lovers needed rather than what they desired. She treated her lovers the way she did her mares, and they all begged for more. What they saw in her, I didn't quite know.

I grabbed Lucyna's saddle and returned to the tack room, figuring Paloma would have left. I was wrong. She stood inside the tack room, inspecting my work as if she were a butler checking for dust while wearing white gloves. Grabbing a bridle, she held it out for me to see. "These will have to be done again. The silver needs a better polish. There's a fingerprint."

I plunked Lucyna's saddle and blanket down on the folding rack, doubting that anyone would be able to see a single fingerprint from a distance when the sun was shining. "I'll take care of it in the morning."

"You'll take care of it now." She lifted one of the saddle flaps. "This is smeared. See?"

I dug my fingers into Lucyna's saddle blanket. I was hot and tired and sweaty and obviously a *thank you* was too much to expect. "I said I'll do it tomorrow."

She lifted an eyebrow. "You seem to have a problem following instructions. Why?"

"Because you're a fucking bitch, that's why!" I grabbed the plastic bottle of leather conditioner and flung it at her. I missed. She didn't.

The force of her hand sent me sprawling against Lucyna's saddle. My cheek throbbed and I coughed as I caught a lungful of leather and horse sweat. My belly clenched. That was the first time she'd touched me, and damned if I didn't want her to do it again.

Thwack. Pain flared on my butt and I yelped. She'd grabbed one of the whips and smacked it smartly against my ass. *Thwack. Thwack.*

"Stop it!" I twisted around and grabbed the whip. Only, part of me didn't want her to. Her gaze met mine and I was hit with a jolt of pure desire. Heaven help me, but she was gorgeous when she was angry.

"Take care of that tack properly."

Adrenaline hit. I shook from head to toe. "I will. *In the morning.*"

She yanked the whip out of my hand. In a low, cold voice she said, "This is my barn. You are my employee. If you want to continue working here, you will perform as I wish."

So now I was no better than one of her fancy mares. "And in what way is that?"

"You're filthy and sweaty. I don't want you near the tack in that condition. Get those clothes off. You're going to take a shower."

"Excuse me?" This was Arizona in the summer. Everyone perspired, including the horses.

Her lips drew into a thin line. "Mares are always so stubborn when they're in heat."

Her voice caused a chill that left me both nervous and aroused. She knew. Damn her, she knew how badly I wanted her attention.

"If you're going to act like a mare, I will treat you like one." She grasped my chin between her fingers. "All my mounts are well-behaved and well-groomed. Either remove your clothes or leave the barn and don't come back."

There was a flicker of hope in her brown eyes, there and gone so quickly I wondered if I imagined it. But for that instant, it was like she could see straight into my soul and know exactly what I needed before I did.

Before I knew it I was fumbling at my t-shirt. Once she let go of me I yanked it over my head. I studied her expression as I pulled off my jeans, bra and panties, but her face didn't change. Maybe I wasn't the type she liked, but I doubted that was it. Her lovers ran the gamut from butch to femme and since I had short hair I generally opted for androgynous.

I stood there, naked, wondering what the hell she wanted me to do next, though I didn't dare ask. She opened a plastic tub full of bits, straps and various bridle odds and ends. Metal jingled as she dug through them.

"Here it is." She held up a stainless steel bit with straps secured to it. "Open your mouth."

At least the bit was clean. I knew, since I'd scrubbed everything in that box. It was cold and metallic and pinned my tongue down. The straps went around my head and were buckled firmly but not uncomfortably. I couldn't talk. At least, not intelligibly.

That done, she wrapped a lead rope around my neck and clipped it there. Then out we went to the wash rack where we bathed horses. It was basically a large shower with a rubber mat and a drain in the center. There were beams on either side from which chains dangled, clips at the end to attach to a horse's halter. She could have affixed them to the rope at my neck, but instead she wrapped the chains around my wrists so my arms were out to my sides and I had no hope of freeing myself.

"Be right back." She disappeared. At least I didn't have to worry about being too cold. Sweat trickled in rivulets down my back.

Paloma returned bearing a bucket laden with brush, sponge and soap. The one mercy was that she used warm water. Even so, I flinched at the stinging stream. She was briskly efficient as she ran the soapy sponge over my arms, breasts and belly, but when she moved to my legs I kept them tightly together.

"Behave," she said in the same clipped tone she used with a recalcitrant mare. Without meeting her gaze, I stepped just wide enough for her to run the sponge up the inside of my legs. Slickness turned to discomfort when she pressed the rough material against my clit and stroked. I shuddered and moaned in protest, but that only made her rub harder.

Punishment...or promise?

Once I was soaped all over, she exchanged the sponge for a bristle brush and raked it against my skin. It burned. I whimpered, and she scrubbed with more force. When she put the brush to my inner thighs, I kicked her leg, half out of pain and half out of the fear of where she'd use the brush next.

Her reprisal was swift. She grabbed her whip and in moments my ass and thighs burned from her swift blows. "You do not kick." Every word was accompanied by a heavy, painful strike. "Understand?"

I nodded and hoped she'd mistake my tears for water dripping from my scalp. She set the whip aside and resumed her scrubbing. When she drove it down the crack of my ass I gritted my teeth and forced my feet to stay planted where they were.

At last she put the brush aside and rinsed the soap away. She took special care when she put the nozzle between my legs, spreading my labia and letting the water tickle my cunt and asshole until I moaned from the pleasurable discomfort.

"Have to make sure every crevice is clean, don't we?"

Nodding vigorously, I angled my hips toward her fingers, hoping she would explore those inner depths, but she turned the water off and freed my wrists. Just the way she'd guide one of her mares, she smacked the whip against me until I went where she wanted—back inside the tack room.

She laid a padded saddle blanket on the floor and gestured to it with her whip. "Hands and knees."

I obeyed, feeling utterly vulnerable as water trickled down my cunt. Paloma rummaged in her own trunk. "You must learn proper posture." With a nylon rope, she fashioned a harness that curled around my shoulders, between my breasts and knotted on my back. She tied this to the bit, giving me no choice but to hold my head erect and bring my chest forward. From the tack trunk she brought out two pairs of leather hobbles, one of which she attached to my wrists.

When she bent to attach the other to my ankles, I kicked.

Her retribution was fierce and immediate. The whip cracked against my ass and thighs, stinging my already tender skin. I moaned and tried to crawl away but she caught me by the harness and shook me until I was too tired and sore to object any longer. I couldn't help but think that she was never so cruel to her horses. At the least sign of pain, she was off their back and inspecting them for damage. Obviously, she had no such care for her humans.

Anger came again, hot and biting. I growled, expecting another beating, but instead she crouched in front of me. Cupping my chin, she said, "This only works if my mares trust me not to hurt them."

She *had* hurt me, but not so badly I couldn't take it. I snorted.

I got another one of those thin-lipped smiles. "Sometimes you have to do what you don't want to because it's good for you. Now behave." Moving behind me, she planted her booted feet firmly between my calves and buckled the hobbles around my ankles. "All my mares learn patience. They wait until I decide what we're going to do." She stepped away and studied me as if she were a judge evaluating form. "Not bad, but you're missing something."

Once more she dug in her trunk, this time producing a horsehair tail attached to a rubbery, phallic end. I shuddered, both excited and anxious about where, exactly, she meant to put it.

I found out when she donned latex gloves and spread a cool, slick lubricant around my asshole. She took her time, coating me generously before sliding a slick finger inside me. "Relax," she said, and I did, breathing deeply as I adjusted to its presence.

Then she took it out and probed me with the firm end of the tail. Slowly she slid it in, filling my body with an alien but not uncomfortable thickness. I jiggled my butt to find it had another side effect. The tail dangled just right to tickle my exposed sex, which set off another round of tingling, aching need.

She cracked the whip against my thighs. "My mares don't show off . They know that all they need to do is stand still because they're perfect just as they are."

I endeavored to do the same, but my wrists and knees were aching from the unaccustomed position and I swayed. With a sigh of irritation, she caressed me from head to shoulder, searching for imperfections and adjusting my stance ever so slightly. Goosebumps rose on my skin despite the heat.

"You're a pretty one. Such nice form. How are you to ride, I wonder?"

Before I had a chance to ponder that, she was astride me, her thighs clenching my hips. She settled atop my lower back. The leather on the seat and thighs of her breeches caressed my skin and I shuddered at the pleasurable sensation. Wetness dribbled down my cunt.

"Easy," she crooned. From her perch, she ran her hands along me in smooth, firm strokes. I felt every shift of her body and moved accordingly, surprised and amazed at how much information could be transmitted through her legs. We swayed and rocked. I arched my back when she squeezed and leaned back when she sat more deeply. My body ached from her weight, but every time I tensed she adjusted her stance so as to lighten my discomfort.

Paloma was good at reading bodies. When she dismounted, mine felt more limber and malleable than before.

She laid another saddle blanket on a tack trunk and patted it. "Up."

Awkwardly I clambered atop it on all fours and she tucked a saddle beneath me. Then she poked me with the whip until I understood what she wanted. My elbows and knees were on the trunk but my hips rested on the curved leather, giving me support but leaving my sex even more exposed.

Of course. Mares were mounted from behind.

She lifted my tail to inspect me. "Definitely in heat." She ran a gloved finger over my clit, sliding it through the gathered fluids. It tickled, but she kept her finger there, swirling it round and round until I whimpered, desperate for her to penetrate me.

Then she moved in front of me, leaving me needy and wanting. She crouched so we were at eye level. With one hand she tucked a lock of hair behind my ear and the scent of my own sex wafted by. I longed to suck the remnants from her fingers.

Her gaze bored into mine. "Don't ever think of disobeying me again. Understand?"

Bound as I was, I couldn't nod. The best I could do was make a sound roughly emulating the affirmative.

"You are my little mare and I will do what I must to make sure you learn." She tilted her head. Soft lips pressed against mine. The slick wetness of her tongue drove into my mouth, claiming me as her own. She was salty and sweet. The bit prevented me from kissing back, or from stopping her from doing anything she wanted. I was hers to fuck or whip or kiss or order around, and I was grateful to have the opportunity.

She plucked out the tail, leaving me with an aching emptiness. She flicked it against my bare skin, lightly at first and then with increasing strength. The horsehair smarted, more so against the tender parts of my arms and calves. At first I flinched with every blow, but then I relaxed into the burning and the stinging eased. She alternated this sweet torture with kisses and caresses, and soon my mind and body were caught in the blissful confusion between pain and pleasure.

She stepped away to inspect her work. "Ordinarily, mares would be able to fight back if they didn't care for their suitor, but I'm not giving you that chance, not when I have to ensure my mares are suitable before breeding them."

A shiver ran through me. I had no idea what that entailed, and I was nervous since I couldn't see her at all.

She set the tail aside and moved behind me. Her gloved hands stroked my tender ass, kneading and massaging then spreading my thighs wide. I clenched, embarrassed beneath her studied gaze. Using her thumbs, she opened me wider still.

And then I felt a soft, fluttery sensation against my cunt. Lips, feathery, smooth and ticklish. I clenched again. Then came her tongue, firm and pointed against my clit. I wriggled, but she tightened her grip to the point that any movement she did not wish me to make was painful.

She dipped her tongue in my fluids, leisurely licking each fold and crevice. She circled my clit, touching, teasing, nibbling until I was breathing hard and moaning. On and on she went, flicking her tongue until my climax surged forth. My body jerked and she drew back to watch my cunt spasm again and again.

"You'll do," she said softly, and let me go.

All I could do was lie there, wrapped in the happy aftermath of orgasm. Dimly I heard the sound of something wet and goopy between her hands. When she touched me, it was cold but quickly warmed. Her fingers had drastically increased their slickness and she coated my entire pussy and ass with the stuff .

When she slid a finger inside me, it was bliss. Two, and it became ecstasy. Fingers squelching, she thrust into me, hands curled to accommodate the curve of my body. She rubbed and wriggled and pressed. A third finger, and she had me humming
with uncomfortable pleasure.

Then she stuck another finger in my ass, and I whimpered. It was almost too much, feeling her inside me twice with only a thin membrane to separate her two hands. She increased her speed, thrusting, one hand, then the other, then both at the same time. My body burned as she spread me wider and dived deeper. I let out a strangled scream as my body contracted around her fingers, clasping them again and again. I raked my fingers against the blanket and my legs twitched helplessly. Wetness continued to flow, and she didn't withdraw until my body had relaxed completely.

Rubber squeaked as she removed her gloves. She patted me on the rump. "Good girl."

Those two words meant the world to me. I'd done well at last, and she'd noticed.

She eased the saddle out from under me and I curled up on the trunk. One by one she removed my tack, starting with the hobbles and ending with the bit. With the metal finally gone, I licked and chewed, just like Lucyna.

A woolen blanket draped around my shoulders. I gazed up at my mistress. Not a single hair on her head was out of place and her clothing remained unsullied, yet my hair was tousled and I was once again sweaty and so exhausted that I pondered piling all the saddle blankets on the floor and sleeping in the tack room.

"You're not done yet."

My mind was too dazed to understand what she meant until she jerked her head at Lucyna's saddle. I let the blanket drop and immediately set to work, scrubbing and polishing, well aware that I was still naked and Paloma watched me.

When I was done, I held saddle and bridle out for her inspection. She took her time looking them over then said, "Go home. Be here at seven sharp." I grabbed my discarded clothes and scrambled out of the room.

The next morning I arrived early to tidy up before the influx of guests and to put one last polish on Lucyna's tack. Then, quite deliberately, I pressed a thumb against the shiny silver nameplate on her bridle.

Paloma would find it. And when she did, I'd be punished.

I was already wet.

TEARS FROM HEAVEN

Jean Roberta

SHEETS OF RAIN ARE POURING DOWN THE PICTURE WINDOW THROUGH WHICH I'm gazing at the emerald green of a well-kept lawn. If hail follows this rain, my flowers will probably be beaten to the ground, but I have no inclination to rush outdoors to cover them with plastic. I have already lost something infinitely more precious to me.

I notice my reflection in my hall mirror just as lightning gives my skin an eerie blue-white glow. My cheekbones look carved from marble, and my lips look taut, although apparently fuller than ever. My brown eyes, looking at themselves, show more clarity than I remember seeing there, as though they had been washed by tears. I haven't actually wept.

I can see the curve of my breasts under a black cotton t-shirt. My Black Watch tartan shorts hug my small waist and my hips like mourning wear for the weekend. For an instant I see myself as the Widow Athena Chalkdust. Absurdity can be comforting.

In my summer break from teaching, I have become unusually domestic. I've been avoiding the university for days at a time, and I hope that my colleagues in the English department can accept my absence as well as I can survive without office gossip and rivalry. Until two weeks ago, I was content with my garden, my books and my pets, human and animal.

Didrick, my able-bodied former student, was my gardener and maid-of-all-work. I watched her planting flowers and vegetables in receptive soil, and the symbolic implications of her work did not escape me. She washed the silk sheets of the bed where I took her, and where her diligence left me wet and fragrant. My poor protégé has never learned to write a solid sentence, but she poured her energy into becoming a one-dyke household staff .

Didrick Bent. The very name arouses such conflicting passions in me that I can't sit still. My house feels empty, but I feel as charged with electricity as the air beyond my walls.

The telephone rings on schedule. She was forbidden to contact me for two weeks, and today is the fourteenth day. I let it ring once, twice, sensing her anxiety. On the sixth ring, I answer.

"Dr. Chalkdust?" She sounds like a child. "You said I could see you today."

"Yes." She will have to express herself without help.

"I really want to come over." The tears that I would not shed are as audible in her voice as gusts of rain on glass.

"You may, Didrick," I tell her, "but you have to come here by shank's pony. Don't bring an umbrella."

"Oh, thank you," she blubbers. "I'm so—"

"Don't say it," I warn her, keeping my voice level. "What's done is done. Your apologies mean nothing, stupid girl. Be here in twenty minutes." She has a long, wet walk ahead of her, but she also has long legs with perpetual wetness between them. Even now, I suspect. The thought makes me seethe.

In due time, Didrick peers in through the glass in my oak door, her hair plastered slickly to her head like the fur of a swimming muskrat. I open the door for the tall penitent, who quickly ducks her head when she enters my hallway. I refuse to let her move past me in her dripping clothes. Her eyes drop to the floor.

"Take your clothes off and leave them here on the tiles," I tell her. I reach for a folded towel in the hall closet, and hold it as I watch her silently remove her t-shirt and denim cutoffs, then shrug out of her wet bra and pull down her underpants. Naked above the ankles, she awkwardly bends over to unlace her jogging shoes.

"Turn around to do that," I tell her.

Her face turns redder under her clinging hair. "Yes, Dr. Chalkdust," she squeaks quietly.

Presenting her firm young bottom to me, she tries to untie her shoelaces as quickly as possible, but I pull out the butt-plug I've been keeping in a pocket, and slip it into her before she has finished loosening the first shoe. I can hear her breathing quicken but she knows better than to protest or to pause. I twist the plug experimentally as she raises one foot to remove her shoe. I know that her movement unavoidably changes the angle of her anus in relation to the plug. I can't help smiling as she repeats the action with her other foot. The plug, shaped almost like a baby's soother, is secure by the time she must straighten up and turn to face me.

My smile is gone when I wrap the towel around her head, bent to receive it, and rub briskly as though to strike some sparks of intelligence into her brain. I run the towel down her body until there are no more droplets glistening on her skin.

Didrick's lower lip trembles. "Ah," I sigh, warning her not to lose control so soon. My warning has no effect. She throws her strong arms around me, almost lifting me from the floor. She is openly crying, and she buries her face in the chestnut hair that flows loose over my shoulders and down my back. "I'm so sorry, Dr. C," she moans. "I never meant it to happen."

Anger flares in me. "Of course not," I answer threateningly in her ear. "You weren't prepared and you lost control. Are you going to live that way all your life, Didrick? What else do you think you might lose through sheer carelessness?"

Her tears are wetting my skin like rain, and the teasing pressure of the toy in her ass seems to be stimulating the flow from her eyes. I gently push her away. I pick up one of her competent hands, now hanging limply. "Come here," I order. "You need to see something."

I lead Didrick to the corner stand, open the glass door and pull out a white porcelain jar. "You know whose ashes are in here," I tell her. "Two weeks ago he was alive and healthy." Two photos in the stand show Pip, my blond wire-haired terrier puppy, romping in spring sunlight.

Didrick is a soggy mess. "I miss him too," she whimpers, holding the breakable jar in obvious terror of dropping it.

"Have you learned anything from that?" I ask her. "You knew he might run into the street whenever he wasn't on the leash. It was your job to protect him until he was trained."

"What can I do to make up for it?" she begs me, sniffing. I take the jar from her.

"Nothing," I explain. "But you still need to be punished for your own sake. Not for his or for mine." Her silence shows a glimmer of understanding. "To the basement," I tell her.

We descend to the permanent twilight below ground-level. I push Didrick beneath a pipe and tell her to reach up. She knows how hard this position is on the arms, even hers, if held for more than a few minutes. I find two wrist restraints on a shelf where I have left them. I climb two steps behind her, and secure her wrists to the pipe.

Without a word, I return upstairs to my kitchen, where I keep a variety of useful things. I deliberately spend some time choosing a pair of black candles, a book of matches, six clothespins with tight springs, a safety pin, a roll of tensor bandage and a large wooden dildo, formerly used for educational purposes in a medical school. I drop my supplies into a canvas bag and carry it to the basement.

Didrick turns as far as she can to watch my approach. I am able to slap the side of her face before I place the bandage around her eyes, cut one end and pin the ends together. Standing on a step, I reach around her to squeeze one of her small breasts, stroking the nipple until it is hard enough for my purpose. Then I snap a clothespin onto it and watch the victim fl inch. I repeat the procedure with the other breast.

"How long do you think your patience will last?" I ask her. "How long do you think it took Pip to die after he had been struck by a car? He was damaged beyond repair. You aren't."

I feel almost naked without a leather belt around my waist. I remember the black one which is still threaded through the belt-loops of a skirt in a basket of dirty laundry atop my washing machine, and I go in search of it. Pawing through my own rumpled clothes reminds me of how far the order of my house has declined in the past two weeks. Threatened by impending chaos, I am relieved to find the belt and to feel its weight as I hold it by the buckle. I want to see the changes it can effect in smooth young skin.

Didrick's anxiety is palpable in the humid room as she tries to anticipate my next move. She expects to be struck. I decide not to give her what she expects. I wrap the belt around my waist and buckle it firmly.

I return to my captive, and casually run my fingernails down the damp skin stretched over her ribs. I press my head into the curve between her shoulder and her face, knowing that the scent of my hair will fill her nostrils. "You deserve punishment," I remind her softly. "but you won't get it yet. It will happen when you're not prepared. Don't you think that's appropriate, my girl?"

The bandage over her eyes is wet. "Yes, ma'am," she whimpers. I pull the clothespins on her nipples, and this makes her squirm.

I part her legs and attach clothespins to her inner labia. I can see her thighs trembling, her solid flesh paradoxically shivering like water. I light the two candles and set them on shelves where they create brave, fragile circles of light in the dusk. I know that Didrick can see them faintly from behind her bandage.

I run both my hands down her belly to her thighs, enjoying the white tracks my fingernails leave on her tanned skin. I know that I don't have time for a leisurely exploration of her body. Quel dommage.

I reach up to attach my remaining two clothespins to the inner flesh of her upper arms. This is to increase her tension, and I wonder if she realizes that it also increases mine.

Didrick's cunt is giving off a distinct aroma as she shifts from one foot to the other. I want to torment her, and I want to bring her relief. I slide down her body until I am gazing into her moist, curly brown bush. I part it to find glistening pink flesh which

moves slightly when I breathe on it.

She jumps when I enter her with my tongue, something I rarely do. I want the taste of her. I pull back when I can feel her hunger, and I switch to another medium. I quickly pull the clothespins off her labia, then reach into her wet heat with two exploring fingers. I scratch her inner folds, feeling for the most sensitive spot which she can't withhold from me. I hold her open so that I can push my man Woody into her, working up a compelling rhythm. A sudden spurt and surrender inside her enables me to bury my weapon to the hilt. She moans gratefully.

I slide my fingers over her clit. She gasps loudly as the orgasm she has been trying to control seizes her in its jaws and shakes her. Her cunt clenches around its hard instructor, weeping with pleasure, as her asshole squeezes its smaller plastic bookmark. She is trembling from her stretched arms to her feet.

I wait for Didrick's last tremors to subside, then I gently remove Woody, who looks coated in wet shellac. I climb up behind her and unfasten the wrist restraints with hands that bring her own smell closer to her nose. Her arms descend slowly, as though they had a life of their own. The movement wafts the perfume of her sweat through the air and sways the candle-flames. I pull the clothespins off her arms. I release her nipples more carefully, but the rush of blood back into them makes her suck in a deep breath which shakes them.

After I have unpinned and removed the bandage from her eyes, I am pleased to see their clear light reflecting the glow of the candles. She is completely covered in a sheen of sweat, and it makes her look more heroic than I remember seeing her before: my thoughtless but loyal Amazon.

I wrap my arms around her. "One more thing, Didrick," I remind her, squeezing one of her buttocks.

"Please, Dr. Chalkdust," she answers. Her voice sounds lower and more mature than I expected.

"Please what?" I tease, reaching for the marker of my ownership still embedded in her anus.

"Please don't ever keep me away from you for this long, ma'am." Her voice reminds me of the blues riff s of several legendary dyke singers.

I reach up to stroke her cheek. "The situation was unusual, baby," I remind her. "I don't expect it to be repeated." I hope she hears the warning as well as the assurance in my words. When I pull the plug out of her behind, she jerks in a way which feels almost rebellious, as though she were unwilling to let it go. I let her see me smile just before I blow out the candles.

In the purgatorial twilight, I reach for her hand. "Didrick," I remind her. "I'm not through with you. Come upstairs for a glass of lemonade while I consider your just desserts." The look on her face is clownish as a grin and a look of fear struggle for dominance.

We ascend to the ground floor where sunlight streams in through my windows. The storm clouds have passed, and no trace of rain remains except the moisture on my lawn and my garden. The weather in this part of the world is as fickle as a child. Consistency must be provided by minds which can think and hearts which can feel.

I pour two glasses of lemonade and hand one to Didrick. I lead her to the sunroom. "Sit here," I tell her, gesturing toward the floor beside my peacock chair. She sinks gratefully to the hardwood and stares into the moon-yellow fluid in her glass. I notice that her nipples are still hard and red.

"I think you've grown more freckles while you've been away," I muse, "if that's possible." Her cheeks flush, and she gains the courage to glance at the mane of dark hair, touched with silver, that weighs damply on my neck. I gather it in both hands, lifting it away from my face. "Didrick," I order, "bring me a hairclip from the bathroom." She seems grateful to have a reason to move, or perhaps she finds my presence too unnerving.

She returns to stand beside me. "May I put it in, Dr. Chalkdust?" she asks sweetly.

"Yes," I purr, amused. She boldly seizes my hair and her luck in both hands and deliberately lingers over her task, stroking. Her touch sends tingles through my scalp and down my spine to my neglected clit and my fasting cunt. Her strategy is as touching as it is futile. "Just fasten the clip, Didrick," I tell her. "You can brush my hair later." She reluctantly encloses my hair in its restraint as tightly as she has been taught, and withdraws from me.

"You need enough work to keep your idle hands busy," I observe. "As soon as you've finished drinking your lemonade, give all the plants a drink of water. The ones in here can't rely on rain." She hastens to obey. She must know how tempting she looks bending over the long table covered with succulents.

"You can see how much still needs to be done in this house, honey." I pet her with my gaze. Before she can guess what I require from her, I further direct her attention. "I need your eyes. Come upstairs and look down at the Persian carpet in the front room from the railing." She follows me like a puppy. I can feel her watching my ass-cheeks as I climb the stairs. How easily she is lured.

When I reach the second floor, I stop. "If you stand here," I explain, "you can still see the stain Pip left. Doesn't it look darker from here?"

She bends over the railing, and I hold her in place with a fist in her hair. My lips are within kissing-distance of her ear. "I won't secure you, Didrick," I warn her, "but you are not allowed to move. Do you understand me?" She nods silently. I hear her swallow.

Didrick's knuckles are already white as she clutches the wooden railing. I remove my belt, grasp both ends and place myself within striking-distance of the two pink cheeks which have been spared for too long. "Count them," I order just before my first stroke lands with a satisfying smack.

The second leaves a trail so red that it will become a welt within minutes. The third broadens the trail. I am not aiming with any precision because I am not aiming primarily for a visual effect. If this is careless love, it serves her well. "Five," she gasps.

"That was four," I correct her. I pause for breath. "And you're not getting the usual six this time. You're getting twelve. With one added for your mistake." My victim groans.

After the first set, I run a hand down one of her burning lower cheeks. She fl inches, but maintains her position. "Good girl," I encourage her. I am tempted to test her endurance to its very limits, but that experiment can wait. I don't want to deny myself for much longer. I leave her in suspense until I see her shift her weight slightly.

I reward her with a crack of the belt which breaks the skin. The raised blood finally escapes, and I hope it releases her guilt as it cools my rage.

After the eighth stroke, I pause just long enough to catch her off-guard when I deliver the ninth. A suppressed scream, flattened to a groan, slips from between her clenched teeth. Her entire buttocks are so crimson that I can't find a neglected spot. To spread my attention as fairly as possible, I aim the next at the underside of her cheeks.

"I didn't hear you," I point out. "How many?" Before she can answer, I strike again.

"Eleven," she gasps. Sometimes she justifies my faith in her capacities. The next two strokes are slightly milder. She counts each one in a barely-audible voice.

I wrap my belt into a tight coil as the penitent begins to straighten up. She looks reluctant to withdraw from the railing because the muscles beneath her tender skin are reluctant to move. I catch sight of her wet face. "I'll bring you a glass of water," I promise, "and you have to drink it all."

When I return from the second-floor bathroom with a cool glass in hand, Didrick has barely moved. I can imagine her frozen in this moment for millennia, like Keats' Grecian urn. I won't allow it. "Straighten up," I command, handing her the glass while pulling her around to face me. "Stand up and breathe, baby. It's over."

I pull her against me and let her hold me. She exudes heat from every pore. "I'll tend your wounds," I promise, "after they've cooled." I kiss her and she responds by pressing her hot mouth to mine. I can taste an intoxicating mixture of anger, fear, relief and lust, with a dash of puppy love thrown in.

As she boldly slips her tongue into my mouth, I taste the strength of the woman she is becoming. I seize one of her hands and place it on one of my breasts, hoping that she can feel my heart beating underneath. "Come," I tell her. She understands me.

In my bedroom, I push her away while taking her glass from her so that I can place it and my belt atop my bureau. I pull off my t-shirt without ceremony. She confidently reaches around me to unfasten my bra, as though she were seducing a teenaged girlfriend. I wonder if she can guess that my body is undergoing a second adolescence, complete with menstrual irregularities and mysterious aches.

Enjoying the charade, I let her pull down my shorts and panties together so that her fingers graze my belly and hips. Her gentle touch is appallingly suggestive. We both know what she could do to me, and that seems to be the most forbidden topic between us.

I guide her to the bed where I slide onto the comforter and lie supine upon it, pulling her into a crouch which requires her to look down at me. Like an animal, she licks each of my nipples in turn. I wonder if she could possibly know what this means to me. Didrick pulls my left nipple into her mouth, and gradually increases the suction. My sighs seem to spur her on. "Baby," I tell her softly, "I never chose to have children." I'm not entirely sure whether I'm talking to her or to myself.

"Mm," she answers, humming around my nipple. She suddenly withdraws and looks at me. "Did you have any by accident, ma'am?" she asks recklessly.

I can't suppress my laughter. "No, Didrick," I answer. "I was careful, as all fertile women should be." She kisses her way down my belly, either to console me for the blood-children I never had, or to remind me that I don't need them.

I am as wet and hungry and impatient as I ever was in my youth. She approaches my core, which is both altar and storm drain, with her usual impudent humility. "Do you want me, Dr. Chalkdust?" she grins.

"You brat," I laugh. "You don't deserve an answer. You know I want you. More than even I can say." I won't say that I need her.

She responds by lightly capturing my clit between her teeth as two long fingers slide into my hot darkness, the inferno which so many fools have sought out. She reaches, she discovers, she strokes. I make no effort to hide her effects on me, and I'm not quiet.

Her tongue massages my captive clit as she fills me, both of us wanting to remain so connected forever. I come with a loud gasp, clutching her fingers inside me as I clutch her head with my hands.

Quietly smug, my suitor waits for my spasms and my breathing to subside, then she slides up and tentatively lays her weight on me, using her elbows like a gentleman. I pull her head down to the space between my breasts. We breathe together.

"Oh Didrick," I sigh. "Nothing can bring my puppy back."

I can feel her spirit sinking under leaden weights of grief, guilt and resentment. "I'm sorry, Dr. C," she mutters.

"You're not following my train of thought, baby," I chide her. "Try harder." I stroke her hair. "I still have you." I can feel the warmth of her smile.

BLEED

Teresa Noelle Roberts

SHE WORE WHITE AND PASTELS, A FLOWING, LONG WHITE LINEN SKIRT AND A simple pale yellow halter. Her high-heeled sandals were white too, and laced up her shapely legs. I thought at first that she looked out of place in a room full of black leather and red vinyl, with her pale garden-party clothes and her rose-colored nails and lips and the nimbus of chin-length fair curls around her delicately pretty face.

Then I met her eyes and realized my mistake. They were gray-green and fierce, implacable as the ocean, a domme's eyes, and they captured me immediately. I held my breath, hoping and fearing she'd make a move. She wasn't my usual type. I'm usually drawn to big butches with chaps and tattoos and bad attitudes, women whose looks signal that they could break me to their will. She was petite, graceful, a definite femme. And she was scarier and fiercer than any three of my former dommes combined.

And that was before she came close enough that I saw the knives: two in white sheaths on her white leather belt. I held my breath as she approached, not sure whether I wanted her to approach me or slink past, twitching those fine white-clad hips as she made her way to another woman.

She stopped, though. Put one small, well-manicured hand against my breastbone, where she must have felt my fluttering heart, sensed the catch in my breath. "I wear light colors because they show blood," she announced, no preliminaries. "Would you like to bleed for me?" Words like that should come out in the sultry faux-Eastern European accent of old vampire movies, between fake fangs, but her voice, like her clothes, belonged in a comfortable Connecticut suburb. That made it far more impressive, far more real, than if she'd embraced all the Goth clichés.

I could have said no. Eerie as this moment was, we were in the middle of a play party, not transported to some dark-fantasy universe where a twisted angel in preppy clothes could actually kidnap me and force me to her will. I could have said no. I could have walked away. And if she hadn't taken that no politely, we had dungeon monitors, like sensible perverts.

Instead I nodded yes because I didn't trust my voice not to squeak.

It's risky to do knife-play with a stranger, but this time I decided to take the risk. Partly because I loved milder forms of knifeplay but had never taken it as far as I'd fantasized, but mostly because of her. If that sea-eyed golden girl wanted to tie me up, whip or spank me, or just have rough but basically vanilla sex, I'd have been all over that too. Hell, she could have wanted to put me in a puppy costume— definitely not my thing—and I'd still have gone for it. Gone for her, because if she had the guts to defy all the norms of the scene, of how a dominant femme should dress and present herself, I knew she'd have the guts to take me places I'd never gone before.

She didn't speak as she led me to a private room set aside for edgeplay that might be too triggery for some people to watch. I was glad, because I still wasn't sure I could force words past the lust that knotted my tongue. Once the door was shut, though, she questioned me about my experience and motives until I forced words together in self-defense. "I know knives as props. Threats. Fear-play. Cold metal on my skin, the dull edge drawing across my throat when I'm blindfolded so the shock makes me come. I've never been cut by a lover. No one would ever do it to me, not even when I begged, because..." Failing words, I pushed up my sleeve to show her the scars on my left arm.

"Because you used to cut." Her voice was non-judgmental, detached, all New England upper-class cool.

It made it easier to nod, and then to tell her my story, as if I were talking to an expensive therapist who did her undergrad at Smith or Wellesley. "When I was a teenager. I got help. I haven't cut myself in nearly thirty years, and I haven't wanted to in about twenty-five. But it's hard to convince someone that I want to try blood-play because I think it sounds hot, not because I'm still broken, and that trying it won't break me again."

The woman nodded and raised the hem of her long skirt so I could see the hatch-mark of scars on her pale, slender thighs, like the ones on my arms. She didn't say "I understand." She didn't need to. But she did say, "One can be strongest at the broken places."

Then she leaned in and kissed me. I hadn't been expecting a kiss. It hadn't seemed like it was going to be that kind of scene. Hell, I wasn't sure it was even going to be the kind of scene where we exchanged names.

The kiss had nothing to with the knives and the menace of her come-on. Nothing and everything. If our scars could have kissed, that might have been more appropriate, but since they couldn't, old pain and darkness touched through her lips on mine. She tasted like cigarette smoke and moss and lipstick and I wanted her even more by the time she was done than I had before.

I still didn't know her name, or she mine. But I let her undress me and lay me down on the cool steel table designed for messy scenes, scenes that might create a biohazard area that would need to be sterilized. She asked if I wanted the restraints built into the table. "Not unless you need to for some reason." I've been tied up and tied down when it added something to my partner's pleasure. Some dominant types love the rope, the cuff s, all those parts of the ritual. But bondage never did much for me, and this time it would definitely take away. "I'm offering myself freely," I explained, sensing that this woman might understand even better than I did myself. "I want to remember that choice every second I'm suffering."

"Then you'll have to hold very still. I will hurt you, and we'll both enjoy it, but I don't wish to harm you. If you move, I'll have to strap you down for your own safety."

I nodded, once again beyond words.

She started, to my surprise, by tracing my scars with her fingers, and from there stroking my body in surprising places: my breastbone, the curve of my stomach, the sides of my ass, the muscled fronts of my thighs. Her hands were small and hard and chilly, but they left trails of fire behind them. Sometimes they tickled as well, on my abs especially, but in a sexy way. The cool, clinical dampness of alcohol rubs, hidden in a white pouch on her belt, followed where her hands had been. I was so aroused that I could hardly breathe, and I had to fight to stay still. Her knives were still sheathed, and I probably could have moved. But if I failed now, she might not trust me when it counted, when the blades came out and the blood began to flow.

I wanted to please this stranger, this femme who looks like a J. Jill catalog, as much as I could remember wanting anything for a long time. And I wanted her knives opening my skin as much as I'd ever wanted anything, period.

By the time she unsheathed a knife, my skin tingled and my head swam. Overwhelmed, I closed my eyes.

She laid the fl at of the blade against my cheek. "Open your eyes," she commanded. "Watch the knife. It's both easier and harder when you know it's coming."

The knife looked like handmade, custom, with a sleek handle, pale wood inlaid with stripes of a darker, reddish one, that fit her small hand perfectly. The blade looked clean, sharp—and absolutely huge from where I was lying, though at the same time a more realistic part of my brain recognized it was smaller than a paring knife.

She started on my right thigh, as if to parallel her old scars. I watched, scarcely daring to breathe, unable to tear my gaze away from that slender, shining blade as she drew it lightly across my skin. Too lightly to cut this time, just a cold, clear line of sensation that resonated up my leg to shiver in my clit. I sucked in my breath sharply, but I didn't move.

She drew the knife over my thigh again. At first I thought it was another fake-out, because I felt no pain, only the cool blade and then a blaze of sexual heat, and I didn't see blood.

The pain caught up with me a second later, sharp as the blade and hot as my arousal, and so did the blood, a fine trickle welling to the surface. My breath hitched, but I was smiling. Sure, it hurt, but it was the good hurt, the hurt I come to play parties to find—and this particular good hurt was better than anything I'd ever imagined.

Better because I'd known that pain before in another context, the way a very sharp blade can cut so you don't feel it immediately, and then the pain blossoms, folding out the way it was now. Only back then that sweet pain was a symptom of solitary despair, of all the ways my teenage life felt like a morass of suck.

This time a beautiful woman was administering the cuts. I wasn't alone. Though I was nervous, I wasn't afraid. And someone's lovely, cool eyes crinkled at the edges as she smiled at how I held still through the pain and pleasure. "Good girl," she said, and though I normally don't like being called *girl*, her approbation stroked the same places the pain had.

Then she cut me again, a thread-thin line of beautiful pain on my other thigh. It was harder to hold still this time, not because it hurt more, but because anticipating the sensation made it more exciting.

Two more cuts followed, one on each thigh. Somehow I managed not to move, but I was moaning now, crying out from an overwhelming combination of pain and lust. "Open your legs," she commanded. When I did, she set the knife down on the table, wiped her bloody hands over her breast, still covered by that so proper lemon-yellow halter. As I stared at the ostentatious stains, she ran her fingers over my pussy.

This time, I couldn't help moving, rising to meet her hand, squirming, begging. "Later," she promised. "Later. We're just getting started."

She took up the knife again and wiped the blade on her skirt.

No dry cleaner in the world would get those stains out, I thought.

Did she keep a collection of stained blouses and ruined skirts, trophies of her various playmates? Another alcohol wipe to sterilize the blade again. I watched the wipe move down the blade and I swear I felt both wipe and knife on my skin.

This time she cut my belly, several tiny, shallow cuts that I'd be feeling for days under my jeans. More blood on my skin, more blood on her clothes, more throbbing in my cunt, more need.

I still didn't know her name.

"The next cut will be trickier for me," she said, "and scarier for you. I want to cut right down your breastbone. Can you be still for that, still as the grave?"

"Nice word choice," I somehow managed to joke, and was rewarded with a sly smile. "And yes, I can. I will."

When the knife touched my breastbone, though, I couldn't help gasping and fl inching. I was ninety-nine point nine percent certain she wasn't a psycho killer, not after the care she'd already taken. The point-five percent doubt was mostly because I enjoyed the frisson of fear or I wouldn't let someone use knives as toys on me. But my lizard brain didn't care about logic. A blade on the breastbone feels dangerous. I managed not to pull away because I knew that would be more risky than lying still for the cut. But the tiny jump, the fl inch, were enough.

"Do you need me to restrain you?" She didn't sound disappointed, just practical, but I found I feared disappointing her more than I did the blade.

And on the off chance she was a psycho killer, my lizard brain informed me, my odds would be a lot better if I wasn't restrained.

Despite her big aura, the force of her personality, I probably had five inches and thirty pounds on her.

Just fantasizing that I might be in real danger made me wetter. While the knife was still away from my skin, I opened my legs wider.

She glanced at the glistening wetness between my legs and smiled like the evil queen in a fairy tale when all her plans were coming together. Then she placed her left hand in the hollow of my shoulder. Her hands no longer felt cold, but as hot if she had a fever. "Steady," she whispered, and I suspected she was talking to herself as much as to me. "Steady now."

She wasn't applying enough pressure to hold me down, but the slight weight reminded me not to move. I watched her face instead of the blade. She was intent, focused, but also flushed with arousal. My breath still caught in my throat at the first cool touch of metal on skin, but I studied her and breathed into the cut, breathed into the pain, breathed into my need.

The thin skin parted and light poured out. Poured out of the cut, poured out of my cunt, poured out of all my old scars like a benediction. My cunt clenched and my mouth opened on a silent scream, but until she moved the knife away and proclaimed, "Now!" I didn't let myself shudder or arch or cry out.

Then and only then did I let my orgasm claim me.

Then and only then did she slip her arms around me and hold me as I convulsed.

When I came back to myself, she kissed me almost chastely. "I'd like to cut you once more," she said, but her voice, formerly so confident and commanding, sounded tentative.

That hesitation, as much as deep-seated desire, made me say yes. But when she said, "Give me your left arm, please," I almost changed my mind. *Not there!* I wanted to scream. Not where I'd damaged myself so many times. But then I met her eyes and saw an old pain in them, one that had faded, but could never be forgotten, one that mirrored my memories. I held out my arm, the scarred underside exposed.

"I want to help you reclaim these scars," she said, her voice low, ceremonial. "Is that all right?"

I nodded, then forced myself to speak. "Yes, please. I've done as much as I can on my own, but I think...this will help finish the job."

Solemnly, she cleaned the area carefully with alcohol. Then, holding my left hand with hers, her grip convulsive, she deftly opened the biggest scar on my arm, the one where I'd cut over and over and again, always avoiding the major blood vessels because I wasn't ready to die but always skirting close because I wasn't so sure about living either.

Her cut wasn't nearly as deep and dramatic as the ones I'd made as a troubled teenager. The scar was numb enough it wasn't painful, and I didn't bleed much, not like I had from the other cuts she'd made. But when she was done and had wiped the blade on her skirt, she took my hand in both of hers and said, "There. I've altered it now, made it something new, part of your present, and I hope a fun part, instead of only part of your past."

"If anyone asks, I can say the scar is from a kinky night with a beautiful blonde stranger who fancies knives."

"Maybe not a stranger. Not anymore," she told me, drawing me into a blood-smeared embrace. "My name's Kate Weston. What's yours?"

EVELYN GETS READY

Annabeth Leong

WHEN EVELYN GETS READY, IT TAKES AN ARMY. Saturday night, the first time I was included in her entourage, she left instructions for me with Beau, her "concierge" and date for the evening. Dressed in a pinstripe suit, Beau met me at the front door of Evelyn's modest but lavishly decorated two-story home. "The safeword tonight is 'red.' She wants you to be the makeup table."

"A table?" I echoed, blinking. I'd been ready for "foot servicer" or even "mirror holder," but being an inanimate object hadn't really been on my personal menu.

I glanced down at my own suit, thinking about how carefully I'd gotten ready, slicking down my hair, packing something special for Evelyn. The table idea made me feel a little affronted. Beau was handsome, sure, with sweet, baby-blue eyes that promised plenty of favors, but I couldn't help sizing her up. I clocked more hours at the gym, had a couple inches on her, and felt a lot of confidence in my ability to handle a cock. I managed not to ask why she got to be the date while I got stuck being the table, but just barely.

Beau clapped me on the arm. "You're a strapping young butch with a broad back, Al. She wants to see how strong you are." I didn't miss the way Beau said she—the word carried the full force of Evelyn's fearsome femininity, but was also laced with enough proprietary intimacy to rub in the fact that Beau, not I, would play the part of Boi Charming that evening.

I ducked my head and nodded. I may not have known how exactly I could be a makeup table, but I wasn't about to lose my shot at being part of Evelyn's preparation. The club night we were supposedly getting her ready for was only a victory lap for her—everyone knew the real party was right here, right now.

"Rita will take care of setting you up," Beau told me before leaving the foyer, straightening her cravat as she went.

Rita showed up seconds later, an elegant, curvaceous brunette who would have made my mouth water if not for the thought of Evelyn. She led me to a room with no furnishings aside from a floor lamp, a thick, soft carpet, velvet wall hangings, for God's sake, and gold and crystal chandeliers. I hadn't thought real people actually liked stuff like that.

Catching my glance toward the lamp, Rita grinned, giving me a glimpse of the white teeth and delicately pointed tongue behind her full, pinup-red lips. "Be glad she didn't cast you as the lamp tonight." Her appraising stare caressed up and down each of my arms. I succumbed to ego and flexed under her scrutiny. "You might have the muscle to hold your arms out straight for her for three or so hours, but as a table, you'll be closer to the action."

Rita stepped toward me, and her perfume flooded my senses with the burnt-sugar bite of my favorite liqueur-laced dessert. She landed one impossibly soft hand on my arm. The more she looked at me with her big, brown eyes, which were passionate and warm despite the metallic colors that glittered on her face around them, the more I started to think that maybe Evelyn wasn't the main event after all. Rita was getting me achingly hard, making me constantly aware of my favorite cock lying against my thigh.

As if sensing the turn my thoughts had taken, Rita rewarded me with another slow, sly smile. Her fingers tightened on my arm. "As the table, you'll have to be good for me, because I'm the makeup girl."

She had to know she'd just rendered me breathless, but Rita showed no mercy. "Take off the suit, stud," she whispered. "Evelyn's going to want a good view."

The way her eyes devoured me had me scrambling out of the suit I'd donned with so much care, tossing it aside as if it weren't my best one. Rita clucked her tongue, and my cheeks heated without her having to say a word. Feeling like a big, messy boy, I retrieved the clothing from where I'd thrown it and folded it for her.

She took the opportunity to look me over some more now that I stood before her in my tank top and boxers. I work hard to look good, but no femme had appreciated my physique with quite as much relish as Rita put into it then. As her eyes traveled, her posture changed, making her body seem even softer and curvier than it had before. I might have been low butch on the totem pole as far as Evelyn was concerned, but Rita made me feel like number one.

She collected the folded suit and walked away. From that view, her thick, luscious thighs commanded the lion's share of my attention. I wanted to lick them.

When she came back with rope and a metal frame, I wanted to beg to lick them. "Get on your hands and knees," Rita purred.

"What's the contraption?"

"I need a nice, flat, very still surface, or I won't be able to take care of Evelyn properly." She guided me into position as she spoke. The frame consisted of four sturdy legs, which she tied my limbs to, and a taut mesh surface that supported my torso and would probably press a pattern into my skin, even through the tank. From the side of the frame near my head, Rita swung out a little articulated arm with a cup on the end. She settled my chin into it. "This way, your neck won't get tired." She patted my head.

The frame supported me, but I quickly learned that it creaked alarmingly if I gave it all my weight. To hold myself solidly and quietly in place, I had to engage just about all of my muscles—arms, legs, ass, back. Rita noticed the moment I found the sweet spot. "Very nice," she said, slipping a hand down to grope my ass.

I wanted to tear free of the frame, pull out my cock, and fuck her hard. The control that prevented this course of action—her instructions, the ropes, and my own desire to please her—made me want to take her even more.

I gritted my teeth as Rita began to treat me as a table. "No more talking until I say," she ordered, smoothing a hand down my back. Then she unzipped a black bag and began removing little jars and tubes, which she arranged in various spots along my spine. I'd never been touched this way by a beautiful woman before, so impersonally with every skin-to-skin contact entirely incidental. Rita didn't try for erogenous zones, and she certainly didn't move as if she wanted to arouse me. Instead, I sucked every shred of pleasure I could from even the slightest brush of her flesh, until my nerve endings felt like big, hungry mouths, and I felt more bound than I had ever been in my life, constrained in such a way that I couldn't express any of the desire that raged through my body. By not acknowledging any of this, Rita fanned the flames hotter and hotter.

Her makeup implements were so cold that she had to have just pulled them out of the freezer, and after a few minutes that sensation soaked through my tank and intensified into a numbing burn. My back muscles twitched with discomfort, and my breath hissed out of my lungs. A sharp smack to my ass shocked a grunt out of me, and Rita laid that displeased tongue cluck on me again. "This table is so creaky and wobbly," she said with mock concern. "My stuff is falling over. Maybe I can fix it."

She fussed with me for a while, tugging at my ropes, pretending to tap something into place here or to twist a loosened bolt there. This translated into slaps and agonizing little pinches, made all the worse since she administered them to the most unexpected places, such as the sides of my stomach or the spot behind my knee. All the while, she kept up a stream of confused muttering to herself, as if it was so hard for a girly thing like her to figure out what to do when she had a problem with her furniture. She even talked about how she wished she had a nice, strong butch around to help her out, and I had to actually bite my tongue to keep from speaking up about all the things I'd like to do for—and to—her.

My body smarted everywhere, and I'd never felt tougher than I did taking all those evil pinches. This table thing was turning me on a lot more than I expected. I liked this game of keeping my mouth shut while a gorgeous woman worked me over mercilessly. It was damned hard, and damned delicious, to take everything she made me feel and lock it up tight in the very center of my chest. It was hot as hell to think about what I would do when I finally got to let it all out again.

Beau appeared in the doorway, anxiety creased across her strong-jawed face. "I'm going to escort her downstairs in five minutes," she hissed at Rita. "Why aren't you two ready?"

"We'll be ready," Rita said, her confidence in my ability despite evidence to the contrary warming me immensely. Her demeanor, as if she expected her words to mold reality itself, affected me even more than her slaps and pinches. I felt myself sliding down into the silent, stolid compliance that I needed to become the table. The pulse of arousal gathered force between my legs, animating my cock until I could have sworn I felt it twitching against my leg.

With an approving hum, Rita finished setting up on my back. My enforced muteness allowed me to dwell obsessively on how I would fuck her if given the chance: what it would smell like, what position I would use, whether she would moan or just give breathy little gasps. I would make her moan, I decided.

116

Then Evelyn swept into the room on Beau's arm, wearing nothing but a short lacy thing, and the air left the room as Rita and I both stopped to drool. I had no choice but to stare, really. Rita had positioned her "table" so I faced the door where Evelyn made her grand entrance, propping my chin up so I couldn't look away without moving and disobeying my directive for the evening.

Evelyn was so exquisite that I might not have been able to move in any case. I almost couldn't believe she was real. A former ballet dancer, she'd kept all her lean, sculpted strength while adding enough weight to fill out her curves. Her hair and features were so fine and flawless, her dark complexion so perfectly even, that I would have thought she'd been Photoshopped if I saw her in a magazine—and this was before Rita's makeup. She smelled of honey and vanilla and expensive things.

Beau seemed ready to burst out of her suit from the pride of the moment. Indeed, no warm-blooded person could have avoided gawking at Evelyn, and I got my eyeful. Still, even with that view in front of me, my awareness of Rita persisted, to my surprise. There was definitely something between us if she could hold my attention even while Evelyn displayed herself with knowing, seductive ostentation.

"I want you, Beau," Evelyn said then, the performance of the declaration obvious in her voice. She knew all of us, Rita included, would have gotten to our knees in a second to lick her pussy or whatever else she desired.

Evelyn groped at Beau's crotch. The butch pulled her into a rough kiss as she fumbled to open her suit trousers. "I'm going to fuck you on that makeup table," Beau promised Evelyn with a growl.

I shivered from both humiliation and anticipation. I wouldn't be getting Evelyn's pussy, I'd be serving as the location where someone else shoved it to her. Once again, that made me flick my eyes toward Beau, measuring her, wondering why she'd been deemed worthy of this honor while I'd been turned into a surface. On the other hand, Evelyn's naked ass would rest against my body, and her juices would drip out of her cunt as Beau fucked her, and gather on my skin.

Rita stepped out of Beau's way and into my line of sight, her ample chest heaving as she watched Beau tear open Evelyn's lacy outfit and suck a nipple into her mouth while she lifted the former dancer off the floor. Rita's eyes flicked toward me, too, though. A few seconds later, when Beau destroyed Rita's careful setup by sweeping dozens of makeup containers off my back, then tossed Evelyn down in their place, I was the one who received Rita's attention. Her gaze was like a finger stroking my face, holding me steady, making my humiliation worthwhile.

Evelyn's sweet, soft flesh felt like lava after all of Rita's cold implements.

I would have grunted if Rita hadn't taken so much time dropping me into the right mindset. Gratitude flashed through my chest as I realized she'd known what she was doing all along.

My fantasies about what Rita might allow me to do to her were only enhanced by the knowledge that Evelyn was currently sandwiched between my back and Beau's cock. The femme responsible for the evening panted as she took what Beau had to offer, but she didn't lose control. "Don't just make yourself come," she ordered. "Fuck me nice and slow and hard. I want you to grind that cock in."

Her legs spread wide enough that they fell to either side of me, almost as if I were the one getting ridden. I kept my breathing shallow, not wanting to let Rita down by being startled into making an inadvertent sound. Beau braced her hands on my shoulder blades and leaned most of her weight onto Evelyn, piling even more onto me by extension. Evelyn slid a little on my back as Beau performed some sort of fancy gyration that forced me to struggle to hold my balance. I appreciated Rita's frame and how well she tied me, because I would have fallen over otherwise.

Focusing on my breathing, I poured my concentration into being a good table, a hard table, a strong table, and was again surprised by the arousal that flooded my body in response to my utter captivity to this strange and arbitrary goal.

"Stud," Rita mouthed at me, and I tried as hard as I could to communicate my lust and obedience with my eyes.

Evelyn's pussy was leaving a wet spot on the back of my tank top and the top of my boxer shorts. She arched up in ecstasy, then fell back down, her skull dropping to my shoulder with a thud that I could feel all the way down to my fingertips. I didn't know how much more I could take, holding myself up under all that weight, and holding myself back from fucking Rita while someone else was getting fucked right on top of me.

Luckily, Evelyn came a moment later, nearly toppling me in the process, almost drenching me in pussy juice, but somehow also managing to talk Beau through exactly what to do to make her orgasm last as long as possible. Beau lifted her off my back a few moments later, and I allowed myself to sag into Rita's frame despite the creak that caused.

"I'd better check the table," Rita said smoothly, coming to kneel beside me. I wanted to kiss her, to tell her that, by now, I was doing this for her, to curl up in her arms and then show her how hard she'd made me. Instead, I held still while she checked me over, untying me, shaking out my limbs, then retying me. She moved efficiently, without breaking the fiction of the scene, but I felt the care in her movements, and the heat that fl owed between the two of us.

"Beau, where's my chair?" Rita asked.

"I'll go get it," the concierge said, and walked off without completely straightening her clothing.

I'd heard about how elaborate Evelyn's preparations could be, and how many players she usually invited, but I was still surprised when Beau returned with the "chair" in question—another butch, tied into a frame like me. Walking behind this new arrival with anxious steps was another gorgeous femme, this one clutching a clear plastic purse full of nail polish bottles. I realized they must have been playing in a different room while Rita warmed me up, and flashed to an image of the curly-haired femme ensconced in the butch's lap, wriggling her ass naughtily to get comfortable in her "chair" while she filed her nails.

Beau set the chair down right in front of my face, and Evelyn seated herself in the new butch's lap, in much the same pose I'd just been envisioning. The nail girl immediately dropped to her knees beside Evelyn, taking one small, perfect foot into her hands. Rita busied herself around me, resetting her makeup bottles on my back, then examining Evelyn's face.

The getting ready began in earnest, and I settled into enduring my bondage, along with the burn of unsatisfied arousal. The effects were made worse by Evelyn's just-fucked musky scent. Her pussy had been placed mere inches from my face—I felt confined not only by rope at that point, but also by all the people surrounding me. She didn't bother to keep her knees together, and I periodically got a view of her still-glistening folds and could do nothing to escape the smell of her highly sexed cunt.

I started to feel antsy, even more obsessed with what I might do with Rita after Evelyn was gone, even more eager to reach my own orgasm, and even more aware of how it might be hours yet before that was allowed.

Beau paced the room. "Sweetheart, how much longer is it going to take for you to get ready?"

"Beau! Now that I've given you what you wanted, you're going to get impatient with me? You know I have to look my best for the club."

They exchanged these lines several more times, and finally, Evelyn's patience snapped. "As you can see, I'm very busy right now, Beau. Everyone is busy helping me get ready. The only one in this room with idle hands is you. So you're going to have to give yourself your own punishment, because I can't do it."

"Ma'am, I'm sorry," Beau said quickly.

"You've had plenty of chances. Go get my hair brush, bend over in the corner, take down your pants, and spank yourself with it. If you don't give yourself red marks, I'll find myself another date tonight."

"Please."

"Do it now. Obviously, you need to be occupied while I finish getting ready."

My eyes widened, though I didn't otherwise move. Beau stayed out of my line of sight, so I had to figure out what was going on by the sound of it. I held my breath until, sure enough, a series of sharp smacks began, each followed by a grunt from Beau. Evelyn exercised such control that she didn't even have to spank her butch bottom herself—she could simply order it done.

"That's good," Evelyn said sweetly. "Really make it sting, baby."

My body clenched in response to the gleeful harshness of her words. I closed my eyes, inhaled the scent of her pussy, soaked up the sound of Beau's punishment, and savored the bite of rope against my arms and legs. Whether Evelyn was ready or not, she'd gotten me more than ready—so far past ready that I thought I would go insane.

For the rest of the time that Evelyn sat before me, I focused on holding still despite the powerful arousal that buzzed through my entire body. Finally, Evelyn cooed over how beautiful her nails looked, and over how well Rita had fixed her makeup and hair. Finally, she allowed Beau to pull her pants back up and escort her out the door. The nail girl dragged her "chair" out of the room, and I hoped they were off to continue their debauchery more privately.

As for me, I finally had what I'd wanted for hours. Rita, alone with me. I wanted to speak, but she'd told me not to until she gave permission, so I waited, still being the table for her. If I'd thought she would immediately pay attention to me, I'd thought wrong. Instead, she puttered about, cleaning up her stuff and putting it away, humming to herself.

She retrieved a tube of lipstick from where it had fallen on the floor, and a soft buzzing announced its true nature. It wasn't until she sat on me that I realized our scene wasn't over—not by a long shot.

Rita writhed on my back for a few minutes, her lipstick vibe no doubt sunk deep into her pussy's folds. I wanted to scream my frustration by then. She fiddled with my clothes, and a moment later she started licking them. I froze, confused by the spot she'd chosen. I didn't have any particular sensation in the middle of my back.

Then slurping noises filled the room, and I realized she was sucking Evelyn's juices from my clothes. The buzzing continued, and Rita moaned. Jesus. I couldn't stand this anymore. I had to have her. It should have been my cock fucking her.

I gritted my teeth, almost seething with arousal at that point, listening while Rita made herself come as if I hadn't been ready to do that for her with lips, tongue, dick, whatever she wanted. I was so caught up in my thoughts that I barely noticed her untying me, patting me on the top of my head like a pet.

"You did a great job, stud," she said, kissing my temple. "You were amazing tonight."

Finally, I could speak. "I'll show you amazing," I growled, intending to grab Rita and pull her into me. My arms, however, hadn't recovered from holding my position for so long. Rita dodged me easily with a little laugh and a shake of her too-pretty head.

"I'm sure you will, Al, but not tonight."

"What? You're torturing me!"

"That's kind of the point, isn't it?"

Still on the floor, I gazed up at the woman I had now begun to suspect could beat Evelyn at her own evil game. This woman had my number. "What do I have to do?" I asked. I would have done anything for a taste of her pussy right then. I'd been dying for it since the moment I laid eyes on her.

Rita slipped a finger inside her panties, bringing it out dripping. I groaned at the sight, closing my eyes in gratitude when she brought it to my lips, licking her juices as if they were caramel. "If you want this pussy, you're going to have to earn it, stud," Rita informed me.

"Tomorrow night, you can come to my place. You can help me get ready. Be ready to work."

I didn't even have the strength to get off the floor. She wrote her number on a card and set it on the carpet beside my head. I lay there gasping, too overwhelmed to masturbate, as Rita softly stepped out of the room and left me there. She was right. The way she tormented me was kind of the point, and I couldn't wait for more.

ANGER MANAGEMENT

Beth Wylde

I WAKE UP IN A CRAPPY MOOD. No certain reason, just one of those things, and I know I have to rein it in before Joan decides to give me her own type of attitude adjustment. Just the thought of what my woman can do with handcuff s and a riding crop makes me shudder. Maybe some early morning sex will cheer me up. My libido is definitely on board with the idea.

I roll sideways to discuss the proposition with my mistress only to find an empty pillow with a note on top addressed to me. Waking up alone and horny with a list of chores only serves to worsen my temper.

At the top of the list is an errand I truly despise: grocery shopping. I know lying in bed all day won't get anything done, though. Joan loves me, I know that for sure, but she doesn't abide laziness at all. If I want to keep the skin on my bottom and have her meal ready on time I need to get my ass in gear. A spanking for fun is one thing but disappointment carries an entirely different type of punishment, one I don't want to experience anytime soon. Once was enough.

My trip to the store is even more hellish than normal. It's Saturday and everyone and their uncle seems to be out shopping. There are too many people and too much noise. Everything is pissing me off . From the overly cheerful girl at the meat counter to the creep behind the register that keeps leering at me. If Joan were with me I bet he'd keep his eyes to himself.

By the time I arrive back home my mood has gone from moderately grouchy to mega bitch. Finding Joan sitting on the front porch swing sipping on a beer momentarily replaces my anger with shock. I risk a quick glance at my watch and frown. I'm late preparing her lunch. My day is about to go from bad to worse.

My Domme stops me at the top of the steps with her patented scowl in place, the one that makes grown men piss their pants. "Where have you been?"

Being the recipient of that gaze is a dead giveaway that I'm in trouble. I know I need to apologize but even the ability to do that escapes me. *What the hell is wrong with me?* Instead I bring her attention to the armload of recyclable bags I'm carrying and let loose with a series of sarcastic comments that seal my fate. "What does it look like? I went to the grocery store. You did want to eat today, didn't you?"

Holy fuck! Did I just say that out loud? Judging by the look on Joan's face, I sure did. I immediately snap my lips shut but it's too late. The damage has been done.

"What did you say to me, girl?"

The question is completely rhetorical and needs no answer. She steps back and points to the front door. "Put those groceries away and meet me in the study. Now!"

The order brooks no argument and I jump to obey. She makes no move to open the door for me so I fumble to get it open by myself and march straight to the kitchen. I've left the door ajar for Joan to enter as well. It's a small start on my penance, but it's better than nothing.

I get a bit of a reprieve since I know she has to go back to work. Whether that is a good thing or a bad one, I'm not sure. On one hand it gives her time to cool down but it also gives us both time to brood over the situation. Sometimes a swift punishment is better than taking the time to really dwell on the matter. Joan can be very inventive with discipline when she wants to be and I'd like to be able to sit down come Friday, seeing as how Joan made reservations at *Elite* for my birthday.

I finish putting everything away and head for the study. Joan is on the phone when I enter so I just stand by her desk and wait.

"Something has come up at home, so I won't be coming back in this afternoon."

Her words fill me with dread. I've really fucked up. Joan has never taken an afternoon off for anything short of a death in the family. Pictures of my funeral dance in my head and I almost miss her next sentence.

"You're a big boy. You don't need me there to hold your hand." She pauses a moment and I can see the mounting irritation on her face. Whoever is on the other end of the phone is about to get their ass handed to them. Her next sentence confirms my suspicion. "God damn it, Tobias. Don't act like such a pussy. You're the fucking vice president of the company. Pull up your big boy britches and take care of the problem."

Her voice has already gone low and menacing, she's in the zone, and since she hangs up shortly afterwards I'm guessing Tobias didn't give her any more crap about her absence. *Oh hell.*

I drop to my knees at her feet and hang my head. It's too late to apologize and truth be told I'm still antsy and irritated. I don't trust myself to speak. My hands clench open and shut in my lap, my knuckles going white every time I squeeze. My headspace is screwed.

"You do know why I'm mad, right?"

I nod, still not trusting myself to speak.

"I can't hear you."

I look up into my Domme's face. "Yes."

Her cheeks redden with rage. "Yes what?"

I swallow hard and force myself to be cordial when what I really want to do is yell and scream and beat the shit out of something. Even my worst case of PMS has never made me this unstable. "Yes, ma'am."

"Stand up."

My legs propel me easily to my feet.

"Bend over my desk."

"Do you want me to strip first?"

She smacks my ass so hard my pelvis bumps against the hard ridge of the desk. "Did I tell you to strip?"

I shake my head. "No ma'am."

"Don't question me, then. I'll tell you what I want when I want it. Now be quiet and take your punishment."

She doesn't start off light. The spanking is meant to be cruel, not fun, and within minutes my pants are down around my ankles and I'm crying and screaming and letting loose all the pent up anger that's been hiding inside me all day long. It still isn't enough.

"Please, please, please." I don't even know what I'm pleading for. I just want to feel like myself again. I know Joan is mad and so am I. Her disappointment in me stings more than any spanking ever could.

"Why, Cassidy? Just tell me why?"

The spanking has stopped. I turn and fall to the floor clutching at her left pants leg as I continue to wail. "I don't know. I've been like this all day long. Something's wrong. Help me. Make it stop."

Joan looks truly concerned as she bends down to peer into my eyes and feel my forehead. "Are you sick?"

I shake my head. "No. Just bitchy." My voice sounds whiny and that just makes me angrier.

My reply earns a small chuckle but I didn't say it to be funny. She realizes I'm being honest and drops down onto the floor with me, pulling me into her lap. I holler when my sore ass comes in contact with her knees. She ignores my yelp and I get as comfortable as I can. My ass is going to throb for days. It was a hell of a spanking. *So much for enjoying my birthday dinner at a fancy new restaurant.* Idly I wonder if her hand hurts half as bad as my butt. I hope so. I'm still sniffling and tears are running down both cheeks. I feel miserable.

"Please ma'am."

"Please what? What do you need?"

I shake my head. "I don't know. I've been in a foul mood since I woke up. I wanted to talk to you about it but you'd already left for work. It's gotten worse during the day until all I want to do is punch someone."

Joan's eyebrows nearly disappear into her hair. "You really have had a bad day." She gives me a tender hug and then moves me out of her lap so she can stand up. "I know just the thing. Strip and wait here. I'll be right back."

She ruffles my hair and disappears into our playroom. I swallow hard, wondering how much more she thinks my butt can take. I really don't want to find out.

She comes back twenty minutes later looking like a totally different person. Gone is her presidential persona along with her business suit and alligator heels. In their place is a white tank top and a well worn pair of black jeans. She's barefoot and the tattoo with my name in it, on her upper arm, is in plain view. Something inside me calms at the sight of that.

Joan's classic hairstyle is now spiked straight up. She's holding a leash in one hand and a collar in the other. My tension lowers another notch as adrenaline begins to override the anger.

She stops in front of me and motions me to my knees. I go willingly. "I know what you need." She buckles the collar around my neck before attaching the leash. "It's been a while since we enjoyed a nice, long session. You're feeling neglected, aren't you?"

I realize she's right. Joan's been busy with work and, yes, subconsciously I know I've been a bit ignored. I know she hasn't done it on purpose, but being left to my own devices for so long has me out of sorts. I nod and butt my head against her thigh. Joan strokes my hair before tugging me along behind her. I drop to all fours and let her lead me. The control is all hers now and I know she'll take me where I need to go.

She pauses just inside the doorway. "I think your ass is probably hurting too much for you to enjoy anything anal, so I'll just have to concentrate on your other parts. Is that agreeable with you?"

Oh, thank God. "Yes, ma'am. Thank you, ma'am."

"Up on the medical table, then. If I'd known your problem earlier I wouldn't have spanked you so hard. You deserved the punishment you got but now I'm being denied your ass." She looks down at me. "I think we're even now." I just smile in reply. "Fair enough, then. Okay, up onto the table and spread 'em. We're going to do something about that nasty attitude of yours. What you need is some anger management."

I get into position, wondering what she has in mind. We've just recently gotten into medical play and since my butt is off limits that also limits Joan's options. When she returns with her little black medical bag of toys I still don't know what she has in store for me. The anticipation kicks up another notch and a little more of my ire dissolves.

I tense slightly when she pulls out the clamps. They could go anywhere. Next comes the suction pump and several cups for it. I have a good idea where she's headed with that. Last, but not least, she removes a small hand flogger and a ball gag. No doubt about the use of those either.

I must look slightly panicked because Joan sets the items aside and begins a slow massage, starting with my ankles and working her way up. She ignores all the parts I want her to pay attention to and spends extra time on my others, just trying to get me in the right frame of mind. It's working.

"Focus on your breathing baby. In and out. In and out. Let all that ugly anger go. Just relax. I'm going to take real good care of you. You trust me don't you?"

I nod slowly as my eyes slide closed. "Yes ma'am. With my life."

"That's a good girl. Now open wide."

The ball gag slips in easily and I grin around it as more of my irritation melts away. Joan has obviously missed her calling in life. Instead of running a Fortune five hundred company, she should have been a therapist—well, a very specialized therapist. It's impossible to stay pissed under this kind of treatment.

The restraints go on next. My wrists are shackled above my head and my feet are spread wide and tied to the stirrups. I'm ready for my flight.

The flogger begins it all. Easy, teasing touches on my inner thighs and the backs of my arms. I giggle when she strokes down my sides and moan when she uses it to slap and tickle my belly. If I could talk I'd ask for more but the request isn't necessary. We're totally in tune and she knows my body better than I know it myself. All I have to do to get her to stop is wiggle my fingers, that's our sign when I'm gagged, which tends to be quite often, but the thought of her quitting is the farthest thing from my mind.

The slaps get a bit harder as she focuses on the top of my thighs and then the area right below my ass cheeks. One blow comes up against the curve of my bottom where I'm still hurting. I shout around the gag and jump. She really did do a number on me during my punishment. My ass is definitely going to be bruised in the morning.

Joan's laugh fills the room. "Just wanted to make sure you're still with me."

The flogger moves lower, trailing over my knees to my toes and the bottom of my feet. I'm wheezing as she tickles them both then groaning as she settles in for several heavy strikes. She knows my feet are extra sensitive and foot play is a big turn on for me. The anger is gone, replaced by sweet pain. I'm almost there.

The sound of the flogger being set aside is loud and I keep my eyes closed, enjoying the guessing game about what is next. There are a lot heavier play toys we have but most of them center on my backside and, today, that is out of commission. I really should have kept my mouth shut earlier on the porch. I won't make that mistake again.

Joan lifts my breasts one by one, playing with the nipples with her hands and her mouth. *Ahhh, she's going for the clamps next.* She nibbles and bites and I squirm and try to beg for more.

"Just relax baby. We'll get there." She takes a moment to put a blindfold on me. "Take a deep breath now."

I suck in hard through my nose and hold on tight to the oxygen as the first clamp is attached to my right breast. The pain is swift and quickly the world around me starts to disappear. It's just me and my mistress and the pain. Before I have time to focus, she's clamped the other one.

"Oh God. Oh shit," I scream, though the words are a jumbled mass of gibberish behind the gag. She doesn't give me any time to adjust to this one either.

She's moved to the bottom of the table. I hear her bare feet against the wood floor as she walks. The rough material of her jeans rub against my thighs as she strokes my legs and murmurs words of encouragement to me. Something cold and slick is being slid deep inside my vagina and I wonder where the hell she had the speculum hidden. *Too late to worry about that now.* She's cranking it open and spreading me wide. Everything I have is on display for her. Just the thought has me wet and panting.

"Is this for me?" Joan rubs her fingers over my opening and I can feel the wetness dribbling down the crack of my sore ass. "So wet. Feeling better dear? I'll bet you are. Let's do some more."

She reaches inside me with two fingers and finds that magic spot, crooking her fingers upwards for easier access. I'm whimpering with the need to come but I know she won't end it this easily. "Good girl. All nice and slick."

The speculum is gone as fast as it was inserted and I know the cups are coming next. I can hardly wait.

The plastic of the large cup is cold on my hot pussy and slips a bit due to the amount of moisture I've produced. Joan just sighs happily and begins to pump the air vacuum. I can feel my pussy swelling as the air in the cup is pulled out. She keeps pumping and I know my lips are huge. My clit too. I can feel it throbbing. If it weren't for the gag, I'd be pleading for some sort of relief. The need to orgasm is overwhelming. *Please, please, please.* I'm begging again, but this time for a totally different reason. My hips are moving with the pull of the vacuum, humping the air. My ass doesn't hurt anymore. Nothing does. The anger is completely gone. I just want to come.

"Mmmphhhhh!!"

Joan chuckles, knowing she's done her job well. I'll gladly agree with her once she finishes me off and removes the gag. I'll tell her anything she wants if she'll just rub my clit.

The suction lessens and before I know it the cup is off and her mouth has replaced it. She's using her fingers to pull apart my puffy pussy lips and locks her mouth right on my clit. I scream. A loud, high, whine as I come all over her face.

The next thing I know the gag is gone, my ass is coated is numbing cream and I'm free from the restraints. I blink and find Joan leaning over me with a huge smile on her face. She's stroking my damp hair tenderly.

"Feel better now?"

I wrap my arms around her neck and literally purr. "Mmmm, yes ma'am. Thank you."

She pulls back and looks me directly in the eyes. My vision is still a bit hazy, though it's clearing quickly. "Good. Next time you be sure to talk to me when you have a problem. I always have time for you. Call me on the cell phone. Hell, you know my office number. Use it. If you smart off with me again I won't be so lenient."

I laugh. I have to. "Lenient? No offense, ma'am, but my ass disagrees."

"Call me by my real name now."

"Sorry Joan, but my ass still disagrees." She shakes her head as she eases me off the table. My legs are wobbly and she supports me tenderly with an arm around my back. We end up in the bedroom cuddling. She tells me about her day and I listen attentively. In return I tell her about mine. There's no anger there now. Just the fleeting buzz of endorphins left over from our session. I laugh out loud at a particular thought I had while we were in scene.

"What's so funny?"

I shake my head. "I was just thinking about how you knew exactly what to do to make me feel better."

"I'm a domme. That's in the job description. That still doesn't explain what was so funny."

"I was thinking you should have been a therapist."

She gives me a confused look.

I pull the blanket up over both of us. "No one would ever get angry again. Not with the threat of your type of anger management hanging over their heads."

Joan shrugs her shoulders and pulls me tighter against her body. "Don't knock my technique. It worked didn't it?"

"Oh definitely. I doubt I'll get mad for a long time."

My mistress laughs long and hard. "Oh Cassidy, you know that's a lie. You're moody as hell. Always have been. Accept it and move on. I have." She moves my hips just a bit until my ass fits snugly against her crotch and her mouth is right next to my ear. The feel of my rear pushed up against her coarse pubic hair stings like hell but I accept the pain as part of my penance and stay still the way a good sub should when her mistress wants to snuggle. "You'll get angry again, probably tomorrow, and when you do I'll be there to manage it."

GARDEN PARTY

Karen Taylor

IT WAS MY TURN TO THROW THE PARTY, AND SINCE IT WAS A LOVELY SUMMER day, I decided that we would have tea in the garden. I am part of an intimate group of women with particular tastes. We take delight in our pleasures, and are comfortable sharing those pleasures in each other's company. I anticipated about a half dozen of my friends, several of whom would be attending with their partners—boys, bois, slaves, the names didn't matter so much. Collectively, however, it was a party for femmes, with their butch companions.

I myself have two, which comes in handy when I'm organizing an event like this. They're as different as night and day, my handsome butches. Jay is built like a fireplug, with steel-grey hair that smells of sunshine and motor oil. She is most often found in well-worn jeans and immaculately polished engineer boots. Austin, on the other hand, is a petite dandy, who is more likely to be found wearing button down shirts, pressed slacks and suspenders that I frequently use to pull her close to me for a kiss.

Their skills are complementary, my butches. Jay is the gardener, Austin the one who selects just the right flowers for the centerpiece arrangements. Austin plates the delicious meals Jay cooks, ensuring that the presentation is always exquisite. Jay keeps our car and motorcycles humming, Austin ensures the chrome is gleaming and dashboards free from dust.

Thank heavens they get along. I couldn't do without either of them.

I watch them through the French doors as Jay hauls the garden furniture into position while Austin consults her seating chart. Their laughter rises and falls through the honeysuckle-laden trellises, and they wave cheerfully at me while they work. I smile, and beckon to Jay. Austin nudges her with a saucy grin, and returns her attention to the arrangement of tables and chairs. Jay stops only to remove her dirt-spattered work boots before following me into my room.

Outer appearances can be deceiving. Jay, with her broad shoulders and blunt fingers, has the lips of an angel. When I am in a gentle mood, it is Jay I call to my room. She kneels before me, gently removes my slippers, and kisses each of my toes. I let my robe fall away from my legs, and she delivers a line of those gentle kisses up my thigh. She is focused, attentive; each of her featherlight kisses convey gratitude. Jay never presumes; she is content if that is all the service I require. I tell her I wish her to join me on the bed, and her voice catches slightly as she thanks me for the privilege.

I think it was that breathless, slight pause, followed by a sincere thank you that first captured my attention, years ago. It still causes my nipples to crinkle. Her wonder and pleasure that she is permitted more access, and more of my attention, is central to her life, and a key to my pleasure.

I have taught Jay how I wish to take my pleasure, and when I draw out my vibrator, she knows that her role this morning is to pay attention to my nipples. She gently cups my breast, and nuzzles lightly as I settle against the pillows. I sigh when she sucks lightly at one nipple while cupping the other breast and drawing a work-roughened finger across it. "Yes, that," I say, and she shivers in response. My rough-hewn butch gently flicks her tongue across my nipple, and I arch my back, purring. When my breath shifts, she shifts as well, switching her attention to my other nipple. The cool morning air against the moisture from her mouth adds to my pleasure, and I murmur "good boy," as she circles the now-free aureole with two fingers. She shudders in response to my words, and her tongue presses harder against the nipple she has captured between her lips. I grab a fistful of her hair, fingers tightening as I begin my first orgasm, and keep her mouth pressed hotly against my breast. Jay moans as I come, keeping her position, and tonguing my nipple until my third orgasm, when she knows from previous experience to stop the stimulation and wait in position until I am finished. I excuse her to her other duties, and she slides off the bed, pressing a heartfelt kiss to my knee on her way out the door.

I shower and consider what to wear. Austin will be in full butler mode, I know—she was thrilled to discover a set of tails at a local thrift store, and loves to dress for the roles she plays. Jay, never a slave to fashion, will merely throw a chef's coat over her shirt while she's cooking. I suspect some of my friends will be in corsets and bustles, the lure of a garden party giving them impetus to dig through their Edwardian wardrobes. I decide on a vintage polka-dotted sundress with a flared skirt, strappy sandals, and a crochet shrug. As I put on the finishing touches of my makeup, I can smell the scones baking. Jay is in the kitchen, and I press a kiss to her shoulder as I head to the garden to inspect Austin's work. Each setting is perfect, the handles of the teacups at just the right angle, the silverware gleaming and just the right distance from the china. Austin is a perfectionist, and I smile as I watch her frown slightly, and fussily adjust a flower in the centerpiece until its curve meets with her meticulous standards. I compliment her on the work, and she preens, showing me the new napkin fold she has learned for the occasion, and fretting about how to keep the tea warm. Austin is my talkative butch, filled with the boundless energy of youth. I chuckle, and return to the house. The furniture has been adjusted in the main room; play equipment set in place, and anchor points in the doorways and ceilings now decorated with sturdy chain and cuffs.

The guests begin to arrive, and offer the services of their companions to assist with the tea. I hand them over to Austin, who is more familiar with the skills and experience of the various butches. She presses them into various duties as I walk with my friends out to the garden. The tea passes pleasantly, with only a few mishaps—a dropped scone here, a cup of too-cool tea there—but nothing that takes away the enjoyment of the afternoon. And indeed, some of the mishaps will be excellent excuses to use the equipment inside after we have finished our poached pears with clotted cream.

As hostess, it is my duty to move the party forward, and so I do. Austin pulls out my chair for me as I rise, and in return, I grasp her carefully knotted tie, and lead her inside.

Austin hates to appear disheveled, especially in front of company. This is, of course, why I force her into such a predicament. She protests, as she always does, claiming the need to finish putting everything away, but she knows she has no choice. I see her cast a pleading look toward Jay, who just winks at her and heads out to the garden to clean up. Austin follows me awkwardly, trying not to step on the back of my heels, color rising to her cheeks as my guests watch her with amusement. I know she is now blushing to the lobes of her ears. I also know that the humiliation is making her wet, and I jerk slightly on her tie for my pleasure.

Outer appearances can be deceiving.

"Please, ma'am, not in front of everyone," she begs, as I point to a padded sawhorse. I enjoy listening to the rising panic in her voice as I order her to remove her clothing.

"Oh yes, Austin, in front of everyone," I answer, and she shudders. Austin groans when she sees that people are coming in from the garden to watch. The attention makes Austin's fingers clumsy as she unbuttons her cuff s, and I yank her shirt out of her trousers, and shove my hand down between her legs. As expected, she is already wet. Good. I step back as Austin folds her clothes neatly and lays them aside. I chuckle, and deliberately kick the pile into disarray as I order Austin to bend herself over the padded sawhorse. She rests her body across the length of it, her legs wide to balance herself. I secure a set of alligator clips to her nipples, connected by a long chain, and draw the chain under the sawhorse, effectively tying her to the sawhorse. From behind me, I hear a hiss of appreciation from one of my guests.

"Look at you, exposing yourself to my guests," I tease Austin, as I pull on a pair of gloves, and then spread her asscheeks. When I rub my knuckles across her labia, she moans in embarrassment and desire. "You are such a wanton slut under all that butch clothing, aren't you?" The gathering audience offers its appreciation as Austin moans again.

"Yes, ma'am, I am," she answers, pushing back against my hand.

"Look how ready she is to be fucked," I say to my guests, shoving two fingers into her pussy. "So slick and ready, I expect you are hoping to be fucked by everyone in this room, aren't you?" Austin whimpers, pressing her eyes shut. I slap her ass hard. "I can't hear you," I say sharply. "What was that, slut?"

"Yes, ma'am," she admits, shame coloring her words. "I want to be fucked senseless, please ma'am."

I strike Austin's ass again, and then rub her underwear across her slick thighs. "I doubt your sincerity, slut," I say sharply, and yank her head up. I point out one of my guests. "Tell her what you would do to be fucked right now."

Austin whimpers, but her eyes stay on the lady, who is smiling broadly. "Oh please, ma'am, I would do whatever you wished if I could be fucked right now! Please, please tell me what you want me to do!"

My friend leans forward, and asks, "What if I wish to see you fucked up the ass?"

Austin squirms, and winces when the alligator clips tighten. She moans, "I will take it up the ass, ma'am, I will take whatever you wish of me, I am your hungry slut."

I smack Austin's ass and say sharply, "Show her your sincerity, slut. Spread your cheeks for all of us to see."

Austin awkwardly reaches back to spread her asscheeks, tears of shame beginning to fill her eyes. "Please," she begs. "Please fuck me. I'll hold myself open, like the slut I am."

There is a smattering of applause and Austin ducks her head, her face burning with shame. But she keeps herself spread wide. I beckon to my friends, and the ladies join me around the sawhorse, stroking Austin's hair, pinching the tender flesh of her breasts, tsking when she squirms, and admiring her puckered asshole.

"You must feel so empty right now," I croon. "A hungry, open hole, that needs to be filled."

Austin whimpers again, and agrees. "Yes, ma'am, a fuck hole. Please fill me, ma'am! Please, I need it so much!"

I tuck my knuckles up against Austin's labia, and rock them against her clit. "I don't think my friends can hear you," I tease her. "Speak louder, slut, let our guests know what a naughty, wanton, hungry fuckhole you really are!"

At this, Austin's eyes open, and she looks wildly at the group surrounding the sawhorse. Her entire body quivers in shame. "Are you really such a hungry slut?" one of them asks her, and Austin moans out, "Yes, ma'am, I am a very hungry slut. I need to be fucked."

"With what?" another asks her. "What do you like to be fucked with?"

Austin's breathing is harsh and fast, as she answers, "Anything, ma'am. I am a hungry fuckhole, I need to be filled, anything will do!" The ladies offer suggestions, from the conventional to the impractical. Austin, poor thing, agrees to all of them, promising to fuck herself on dildos, police batons, wine bottles, whip handles, cucumbers, table legs, and even her motorcycle tail pipe.

"How about my hand?" I suggest, pressing my knuckles against her pussy again.

"Oh yes, please, please ma'am, I can take your whole hand!" Austin cries urgently, pushing hungrily back to me.

"That's right, slut," I encourage her. "Show my nice friends what a hungry fuckhole you really are. Fuck yourself on my hand," I order her, as I slide two, then three, then four fingers into her soaking pussy. "Tell them how much you need this."

Austin's strangled cry as she pushes back onto my hand is almost enough to make me orgasm, but I keep myself focused, and remind her to speak while she fucks.

"Oh fuck, fuckity fuck," she pants as she and I work together, sliding my hand fully inside her. "Hungry fuckhole, I am a hungry fuckhole," she pants, grinding herself on my fist. "Such a slut, slut, fuck, fuck, slut, yes, fuck!" she cries, I chuckle as her words begin to fail her, and she collapses into grunts, rocking back onto my hand, fucking herself for our audience. She is arching her back, the clamps tightening on her nipples as she does. She screams, but the pain seems to drive her even closer to the edge of orgasm.

I grin, and begin to chant, "Come. Come. Come!" My friends join in enthusiastically, surrounding Austin with a chorus that serves to remind her that she is the center of attention at this party. "Come, Come, Come!" we chant together, and she begins to buck and grind, howling as her body shudders and her cunt clamps down hard on my hand. She comes in waves, her body spasming as the group starts to applaud, her embarrassment forcing yet another orgasm.

When Austin slumps in exhaustion against the padded sawhorse, I ease my hand from inside her. Our audience drifts away, inspired to try other pieces of the playroom's equipment, and soon the room is filled with the sounds of women playing, fucking, and coming. I gently release Austin from the nipple clamps, and she slides off the sawhorse into a pile of exhausted flesh at my feet. I allow her to lean groggily against my shin while I talk with a few of my guests. When I determine that she is able, I order Austin to gather up her clothing, and return to the kitchen. She presses a grateful kiss to my knee, and disappears. After a short break, she returns to the playroom, fully dressed, looking cool and collected, and carrying a tray of beverages for my guests.

The party breaks up a few hours later. Austin fetches missing purses and sex toys, while Jay brings the cars around. I kiss my guests on the cheek, thank them for attending, and we promise we will see each other soon.

Fireflies are dancing in the garden as the last guest leaves, and the air is filled with the smell of honeysuckle and the sound of crickets.

With a pleased sigh, I close the French doors and head inside. My butches have nearly finished putting the great room back to its original shape, and I sink into a chair, waving for them to finish their work. They join me when they are finished, Austin bringing a tray of drinks for the three of us, and Jay kneeling, hands resting quietly on her thighs. I thank them both for making me look so good, and they glow with pride. We begin to talk, Jay shifting over to remove my sandals and massage my feet, Austin brimming over with ideas about costumes for the next gathering, which will have a Halloween theme.

I gaze at them, my two handsome butches, so different from each other, and so different on the inside than they appear on the outside. Together, we are complete.

PRIMA

Katya Harris

"NO, NO, NO!"

Stalking over to the sound-system, Ilona turned it off with a sharp jab of her finger. Jenna flinched, her ears ringing with the sudden silence.

Spinning round, her ankle-length skirt flaring wide, Ilona moved toward Jenna. Her features were expressionless, her emotions hidden by a mask of unnerving impassiveness. She rarely looked different. Decades of training and dancing had carved her face into a mask of serenity, untouched, except for when she was performing or experiencing the most extreme emotions. It was her body that betrayed her and she was clearly furious. She walked toward Jenna, leashed fury in her every fl owing movement. Jenna shivered, her hands clenching tight around fistfuls of her short chiffon skirt, ruining the fine fabric. Her heart, already rapid with exertion, rabbit-kicked against her rib-bones.

"Is this what you call dancing?" Ilona seethed. She prowled around Jenna who was frozen to the spot in the middle of the studio. She didn't wait for an answer. "You are meant to be a swan." Her hair flicked against Jenna, a thousand silken whips, as she started to dance around the younger woman. "Elegant. Graceful. Every movement effortless, as if your body is nothing but an extension of the music." Ilona didn't even need the music to dance like that; she carried it within her. Not for the first time, a pang of envy plucked at Jenna's heart.

Stopping in front of her protégée, Ilona sneered at her, the slightest lifting of a thin red lip. "You are like a pig in the barnyard."

"I'm sorry, Prima," Jenna said quietly, trying not to show how deeply Ilona's criticism cut her. She had spent days practicing this piece, dancing till her feet bled. "I'll do it again."

Making a rude noise, Ilona looked Jenna up and down before her eyes settled on her face. "No. I can't bear to watch you anymore," she declared. "Your incompetence off ends me. I don't even know why I bother with you."

Jenna's stomach dropped to the floor. Panic chilled the sweat that glazed her skin. "No, Prima. Please. I'll try harder."

Ilona's eyes gleamed, chips of obsidian in the pale whiteness of her face. "I have seen your best and it is not good enough. I'm wasting my time with you."

"Please Prima," Jenna begged. Tears welled in her eyes and fell in fat drops down her cheeks. Her chest felt so tight she could barely breathe. Oily desperation twisted in her stomach and with only a fleeting thought of her dignity, she dropped to her knees in front of the other woman. Humiliation washed through her, a wave of heat that singed her, but she didn't move as she looked up at that unyielding face. "I can do better, I know I can. Prima, I'll do anything. Anything you want. Just give me another chance. Please."

In her youth Ilona had been one of the most accomplished prima ballerinas in the world. Since she'd retired, she spent her time fostering the next generation of talent. To have her as a mentor meant everything to Jenna. The last two years had seen her become one of the main dancers of a small, but prestigious dance company, and she was even being touted as an up-and-coming star. She was twenty-one years old and all her dreams were coming true, and Jenna knew she would never have achieved half as much if it weren't for the woman staring down at her now.

The smile that stretched Ilona's blood-red lips was not pleasant. Leaning forward, she twisted a hand in Jenna's hair, pulling it tight. Jenna cried out and then again as Ilona forced her head down to the floor.

"If you're going to beg, my dear, then do it properly."

Jenna sobbed. Her hands flexed on the floor. Shame stained her skin red, but she did what Ilona wanted. "Please Prima. Please let me try again. Please let me stay. I promise, I will do anything you want me to do. I swear it, just don't give up on me." More tears tumbled from her eyes, splashing on the floor beneath her face. Ilona's bare feet were just by Jenna's head, her hand still buried in Jenna's hair. With a lurch that yanked her hair painfully, Jenna pressed her lips to first one foot and then the other.

"Is that the best you can do? Your begging is even worse than your dancing."

Ilona's derision lashed at Jenna.

Skin flaming, Jenna opened her mouth. She kissed Ilona's feet as if she were kissing a mouth, her tongue even dipping into the sensitive spaces between Ilona's toes.

"Mm, a little better," Ilona purred. "But I think you could do with a lesson."

Jenna stilled. When Ilona moved away from her, letting go of her hair, she stayed where she was. The breath shuddered from her lungs, and she whimpered when she heard Ilona's soft footsteps come back toward her.

"Bottom up."

Jenna sucked in a breath, letting it go in a steadying stream. Slowly, she tucked her knees under her, lifting her bottom into the air.

Her skirt lifted, was folded back to drape around her waist. Long nails scraped across her buttocks as Ilona tugged the seat of Jenna's leotard into the crack of her bum. She pulled it tight, so the thin material separated the lips of her pussy too. Jenna yelped as it rubbed against her clit with a jolt of sensation.

"There," Ilona said, giving her a little pat on the bottom.

Something made a swishing noise through the air. Jenna was breathing so loud she barely heard it. She didn't have time to brace herself when the first blow landing on her left buttock, swiftly followed by one to her right. Two quick flicks. Pain exploded across the toned flesh of her ass, bursts of stinging flame. Jenna's surprised cry echoed through the quiet studio. Her hands curled into fists beneath her chin.

"Shall I continue?"

Licking her dry lips, Jenna meekly said, "Yes, Prima."

The riding crop cut through the air with a whistling shriek. Jenna knew what it was. She had felt its kiss many times. It was Ilona's favorite instrument.

Pain flared and popped across her ass. It rippled outward across the surface of her body, wave after wave of sharp-edged sensation. Each cresting peak forced a noise from her slack mouth. Gasps, groans, squeals and screams. Jenna couldn't keep them in, and she couldn't keep still either. She squirmed and wriggled, helpless little movements that had her reddening bottom wiggling in the air.

"Shameful," Ilona hissed as she wielded the crop with an expert hand. Each blow was precise, the rhythm unrelenting. "How many times do I have to punish you? You think you are a dancer, but all you are is a shameless little slut. You don't care about the dance. You only care about what's between your legs. Isn't that true?"

Jenna sobbed. "Yes, Prima." Her ass felt huge, a swollen lump that throbbed with blazing heat.

Ilona snorted. The blows stopped. The fl at end of the crop stroked over the tortured globes of Jenna's ass. It made her squirm even more.

The crop slid lower. "Are you wet?"

Jenna moaned. She didn't know which of her cheeks were redder, her ass or her face. "Yes," she whispered.

The crop stilled. Only her leotard kept it from touching the swollen pearl between her pussy lips directly. Jenna froze at the silent threat. She gulped, remembering.

"Yes, Prima."

A fraught moment and then the crop moved, slipping between Jenna's plump labia. Jenna bit her lip to keep from moaning or from pressing back to deepen the too light touch. When the tongue of the crop rubbed teasingly over her clit, tension sang through her body. She wished she was naked.

Pleasure tingled up Jenna's spine, mixing with the pain throbbing from her abused bottom. She gasped, a bone-deep shudder wracking her body. If she moved just a little, just a small circle of her hips, she would orgasm. She could feel the pressure of it, a heavy weight glowing in her belly.

"You want to come, don't you?" Ilona crooned. It didn't surprise Jenna that the other woman knew. Ilona had long ago learned all her secrets.

"Yes, Prima." The words came out with a moan, an abject sound, because Jenna couldn't deny it. She wanted to wallow in the shame-fuelled pleasure of her Prima's touch. If she hadn't known that Ilona would just extend her torment in retribution, she would have been tempted to steal the orgasm.

"Well I don't want you to," Ilona purred. "You won't, will you?"

"No, Prima." Jenna's fingers curled into her palms. She hoped she wasn't lying.

"Hmm, let's see."

The light tap of the crop against her clit sent shockwaves of pleasure through Jenna. She gasped in a breath and then released it in a long drawn out groan. Her fingernails bit into her palms as her fists clenched hard. Another slap had her shaking with the effort to stave off the climax building with ferocious force in her groin.

"Good. Good." Ilona's voice flowed over her like warm honey. "Just a few more."

Jenna groaned. "Yes, Prima."

Three more soft blows landed on her pulsing clit. Jenna counted them out in her head, only managing to hold off her orgasm by the skin of her teeth. Sweat slicked from her body. Her breasts heaved with the force of her breaths, her hardened nipples raking against her knees. She couldn't stop shaking.

"Very good." Ilona's tone was one of warm approval. It suddenly chilled with her next words. "Now if you would only be so disciplined when you're dancing."

The criticism cut deep. "I do my best, Prima," she protested softly, frustration loosening her tongue. "It's difficult."

The beat of silence that filled the studio had the sweat cooling on Jenna's body in sudden dread.

"You're giving me excuses?" Ilona hissed.

Jenna shook her head, her hair shimmering around her with the violence of her denial. "No, Prima."

"So you are arguing with me?"

Another shake of Jenna's head. "No, Prima."

The flat of a foot pushing on Jenna's side sent her sprawling, face-up, on the floor.

Ilona loomed over her. She tapped the tongue of the crop against her own calf. Once. Twice. Her dark eyes gleamed, and Jenna knew the other woman was enjoying the fear and anticipation she couldn't hide.

Jenna flinched when Ilona tossed the crop aside. It clattered across the floor.

The whisper of Ilona's clothes hitting the floor made Jenna shiver.

Ilona hadn't danced professionally in years, but her body was still a thing of lithesome beauty. Jenna's breath caught, and she couldn't stop herself from caressing Ilona's long limbs and toned body with her eyes. Her hands itched to follow suit. Juices trickled from her overheated cunt, soaking the crotch of her leotard even more.

With the tip of her right big toe, Ilona pushed on Jenna's shoulder until she lay fl at on the floor, her knees spread wide. The polished wood was cool beneath her, but it warmed quickly from the heat of her body.

Ilona straddled Jenna's head, facing down her body. She went to her knees, her pussy positioned directly over Jenna's face. The familiar smell of Ilona's arousal surrounded her, salty and musky. The sight of her slick pussy, the puff y outer lips and frilly inner lips, the fat knot of her visibly throbbing clit, sent Jenna's arousal into the stratosphere. She wanted to lift her head and bury it in all that sweet, soft flesh, but Ilona kept herself just out of reach.

"Do you want to lick me, my greedy little slut?" Ilona cooed.

"Yes, Prima." Jenna was so desperate to do just that, she couldn't keep still. She twitched with her need.

Bracing her hands on the floor, Ilona lowered herself a little. Jenna raised her head, stuck out her tongue as far as she could, but she still couldn't reach that succulent pussy.

"Mm, I don't think you deserve to. You are a little pig after all." Looking down her body at Jenna, Ilona wasn't impassive anymore. Her eyes glittered like black diamonds above her flushed cheeks. Her body shifted, drawing Jenna's eyes back up. The dark rosette between the crack of Ilona's bum cheeks winked down at her. "Lick my asshole. Lick it like the dirty piggy you are."

Ilona lowered herself down, slowly, giving Jenna plenty of time to protest, to choose not to. She knew that Jenna wouldn't decline. It was just one of a hundred little ways to remind Jenna that she wanted to do these things not only because she worshipped Ilona, but because deep-down it was what she wanted.

Furious red burned in Jenna's cheeks, not with anger, but with the strength of her shame. It was the most degrading of acts, but it still made her lust burn hotter and without even thinking about it, her tongue was snaking out. Curling her arms up and around Ilona's thighs, she used her hands to pull apart her ass-cheeks, and, taking a deep breath, buried her face between them.

Jenna flickered the tip of her tongue over the tightly furled ring of her mentor's bum-hole. With Ilona's thighs pressed against her ears, she could barely hear anything, but she caught her Prima's moan. She kissed the flexing pucker of Ilona's bottom, lavishing the nerve-rich flesh with attention. Beneath her hands, Ilona's thighs quivered, and Jenna's open lips pulled upwards. She may have been the one with her mouth on the other woman's anus, but she had the power to make Ilona tremble.

A splat of liquid hit Jenna's chin. Another landed on her neck, dribbling down the sensitive skin—the dripping wet evidence of Ilona's lust. The last little bit of Jenna's control snapped.

With an abject moan, Jenna laved Ilona's bum-hole with the flat of her tongue. She mouthed it, kissed it and when she felt it soften beneath her ministrations, she thrust her tongue inside it.

Ilona groaned. Leaning back as she widened her knees, she rode Jenna's mouth, helping her pump her tongue deeper into her ass-hole.

"That's it," Ilona growled. "Fuck my ass. Fuck it hard, you filthy little pig."

Jenna did, languishing in the dirtiness of the act. Her clit throbbed, a demanding drumbeat between her legs. She wanted to reach down, to sink her own fingers into the wetness of her pussy and bring herself off as she did the same to Ilona. Her Prima hadn't given her permission though, and she knew this was just as much punishment as her whipping.

Fingers brushed against her chin as Ilona started fingering her own pussy, her honey dripping onto Jenna's neck. Groans turned to sharp-edged cries; Ilona was going to come and soon.

Ignoring the ache in her jaw, the increasingly acrid taste of Ilona's bottom in her mouth, Jenna thrust her tongue even deeper. She moved it in the tight tube of Ilona's rectum, waggling it back and forth. Anything to please Ilona, to push her over the edge of orgasm. Maybe if Jenna did it well enough, she would get her own satisfaction.

Undulating madly, Ilona ground her butt down so hard it was difficult for Jenna to breath. The muscles in her thighs jumped and twitched against Jenna's head, the squish of her fingers pumping in and out of her pussy loud in Jenna's ears. "Oh yes, that's it. You're making me come, you dirty little bitch!"

Shattered cries bounced around the room. Shoving her tongue deep into Ilona's rectum, Jenna flexed it as her Prima rode out her orgasm, screaming and shaking. A gush of wetness flooded over Jenna's chin and throat. Slipping her tongue free, she frantically licked at Ilona's come, drowning in the musky-sweet taste.

Breathing hard, Ilona moved to kneel at Jenna's side. Her face was flushed, her eyes bright. The red of her lipstick had smeared around her mouth. Her black hair with its distinctive streak of white at her right temple was wild and tangled down her back.

Leaning forward, she brought her face to within a finger's width from Jenna's.

"What a good little piggy you are," she crooned. Her nose wrinkled. "Messy, though." Her eyes tracked over Jenna's face.

Jenna couldn't help but squirm with the force of her arousal. "Yes, Prima."

Lifting a hand, Ilona brushed the back of her fingers against one of Jenna's pouting nipples. Jenna whimpered.

"Please, Prima," she begged.

Capturing Jenna's nipple, Ilona squeezed it between her thumb and forefinger. She compressed the tender peak until Jenna cried out, the pleasurable pain of it shooting straight to her clit. Her feet kicked out as much with the intensity of the feeling as with frustration. It wasn't enough to make her come.

"No," she wailed when Ilona released her. "Prima!"

Ilona leaned in closer, her mouth by Jenna's ear. "If you want to come, then dance."

She flowed to her feet, grace and poise in every movement. Jenna's rise was not so well coordinated. She felt clumsy, her body heavy with her unsatisfied arousal.

Scooping up her clothes, Ilona walked back over to the stereo.

Placing her finger on the play button, she turned and faced Jenna. "Do the last sequence perfectly and then you'll get what you want." Her lips tilted up. "Are you ready?"

It was useless to argue. Jenna gulped and assumed the start position. Taking a deep breath, she held it for a second and then released it. "I'm ready, Prima."

"Then dance, and let's see if my piggy can turn into a swan."

The music started and Jenna danced.

THE RIDE

Kathleen Delaney-Adams

HER OWN CUNT COULD TAKE A GREAT DEAL BIGGER THAN THIS, ERIKA reflected as she slid her slender, candy-pink cock between Baby Butch's butt cheeks. She smiled a bit smugly at her newfound and squirming plaything. Despite the fact that his jeans were now pushed down somewhere around his ankles, despite being bent over with his ass in the air and sex exposed, Baby Butch appeared to be in the throes of some sort of animalistic heat. Grunting and writhing on Erika's small dildo in the parking lot of the station, he seemed to have completely forgotten that an hour ago he still had his clothes on and his dignity intact.

She had been toying with Baby Butch for weeks. Startlingly fresh-eyed, he was no older than thirty, and not remotely her type. Baggy-boy jeans and white t-shirt and puppy dog eyes did not do it for her, and other than the *very* occasional love tryst here and there, she never went for dykes. It was the salt and pepper executives who dominated Erika's professional life that moistened her fantasies. The power-types who sauntered coolly into board meetings, exuding dignity and money and disinterest. Until, that is, she demanded their attention and respect—and yes, *lust*—the moment she stood in her spiky stilettos and commanded the meeting. She adored the way she could floor them with a well placed glance, shame them with her cold and thorough analysis, watch their cocks swell, literally, when she moved through the room, allowing her ass to swish just a bit and never enough to appear unprofessional, rattling off numbers and percentages. She never accepted their offers to take her out or keep her in, never accepted their phone numbers, and certainly never gave them hers. It was too messy, and she abhorred a mess, preferring her immaculate, controlled life and pristine appearance. Well-kept and highly maintained did not leave much room for sleaze, and on

149

the occasions Erika allowed herself a spontaneous lustful tryst she always did the fucking, keeping it clean and anonymous. Finding guys who were okay with that on every level was a rare treat indeed, and her last rendezvous was becoming a hazy memory.

Then along came Boy Toy with his baseball cap and loose walk, and damn but she was inexplicably hot for him. She longed to teach him that just-laid-a-girl swagger, ached to smear his mouth with cunt juice and lipstick, and jacked off at the thought of bending him over her knee and spanking the hell out of that fine tight ass of his until he was sobbing and begging for more of it. Her morning commutes on the train were becoming downright sticky and dangerous. Many a morning after riding in the same car with Baby Butch, Erika arrived breathless at the firm, told her assistant to hold her calls, locked the door of her spacious top floor office, and fucked her pussy with her red tipped fingers—or used one of the array of dildos and vibrators and cocks she kept in her desk drawer for when she was really dying to get off hard.

It started sweet and casual enough, Baby Butch meeting her eyes with a shy smile, her own smile merely polite in response. It didn't take long for Erika to notice him sidling closer to her on the platform of the train, staring at the ground somewhere in her vicinity and blushing furiously. It was *cute*. Cute in that puppy way. And becoming decidedly cute in that "ooh, he-might-be-fun-to-toy-with" way. She began pouring the flirt on just to see his reaction. Squeezing behind him so her pussy rubbed across his ass, touching him lightly on the arm as she passed, oozing sweetness and charm as she murmured, "Hi, doll," in his ear. She got off on watching him squirm and stammer, so much so that it was just a matter of time before she decided to up the ante. Erika wanted to see exactly how much this Baby Butch could take, and if her own interest had peaked beyond idle fun, she would certainly never admit to it.

During a somewhat dreary Monday morning commute, Erika made her move. The train was packed with the usual rush hour crowd, and she elbowed her way through the throng to press tight up against the back of her blissfully unsuspecting target.

"Don't turn around," she cooed, her lips brushing against his ear.

Baby Butch started, then remained still. Erika had to give him credit. She could feel his breath quicken but he never turned around. She slid her well-manicured hands slowly around his waist, stopping at his belt buckle. A pause. An eternity. She felt her own excitement start to build as moments ticked by, waiting until a slight whimper escaped from Baby Butch's mouth.

Erika slid her hand down the front of his jeans, surprised to discover he was packing. Hard. Is *this* how dykes rolled these days? Mmm, nice. She grabbed and squeezed at him, rubbing his cock first gently then, glancing around and realizing no one was paying the slightest attention to their antics, she allowed herself to pull harder on him. When his hips began to rock in rhythm with her strokes, she stopped. Gave him just a trace of her finger down the long length of his package. Smiled to herself when she felt him squirm in response.

She undid his belt buckle stealthily, loosening his jeans just enough to slide her hand into the back of them. The fact that he wriggled a bit to give her greater access did not go unnoticed.

Without warning, Erika slid a long manicured finger into his ass. He jumped, shocked, and cried out loud enough to garner the glances of a handful of curious travelers.

"Shut up," Erika hissed.

Baby Butch remained stiff with tension but clamped his mouth closed. Erika waited to feel his body relax a bit before she began to move her finger, sliding in and out of his asshole. She knew he was giving in to her when he again began to rock, moving with her finger. When his hips rocked faster, Erika increased her own tempo, coming out completely to spit on her fingers before shoving two back in, again and again. He moaned low in his throat and she knew he wanted her, wanted this done to him. She felt her own pussy become creamy with hunger, a liquid fire dampening her thighs and flushing her face. Later. She would get off later, now was all about him and making him writhe with need for her. She found herself exhilarated by this more than she had anticipated. A ball-breaker professionally and personally, she was used to being bowed down to by men and women alike. But *this?* Demanding her right to take this young butch, laying claim to him publicly? There was something sweetly victorious about it that made her cunt juice and thicken with her own aching need.

Suddenly Baby Butch began to tremble, his eyes closed. Abruptly, Erika stopped finger fucking his ass, withdrawing her hand and wiping her fingers tidily clean on the lace handkerchief she carried.

"I didn't say you could come." Her voice was low, calm, chastising. Disappointed in him.

He immediately began stumbling over himself in a hasty attempt to apologize. Erika held her hand up to stop him.

As the train pulled into Arlington Station, Erika realized she was not done with him yet. Thank god she kept her cock in her briefcase for emergencies such as these; it had been a lifesaver on more than one occasion.

"I'm getting off here. Follow me." Her tone brooked no argument. As she stepped gracefully onto the platform, she glanced over her shoulder, pleased to see a flustered Baby Butch fumbling with his belt as he hurried after her.

Erika stepped outside into the cool breeze and turned the corner of the building, her heels tapping decisively on the pavement. There were people scattered throughout the parking lot of the station, but she chose to ignore them. Her need to take him here and now, to drive him to his knees before her, could not be resisted. She lusted for this young boi who now stood before her, offering himself deliciously and completely to her. He stopped in front of her and waited, eyes on the ground, hands folded in front of him. She could almost hear his pulse pounding.

"Good." Erika threw him a bone, enjoying the blush that heated his cheeks at the praise.

She set her briefcase down and unzipped it, taking her pale pink strap-on out of the side pocket and relishing the way Baby Butch's eyes widened. It was already in its pink leather harness, and Erika stepped easily through the leg straps and drew it up her long lithe body and over her hips. She allowed him to watch, noticed the way he took in her legs, the bit of lace at the top of her stockings, the way her tight skirt rode up over her hips when she put the harness on. A glimpse of delicate thigh, a peek at her garters—by the time she was strapped and ready for him he was once more gasping for breath.

Just you wait, Erika thought.

"Drop your pants," she commanded.

As if the thought to deny her never even crossed his mind, Baby Butch complied immediately, dropping his jeans to the ground around his ankles. His hand on the waistband of his briefs, he raised his eyes at Erika's questioningly. At her nod, those, too, were pulled down, leaving his cock and cunt exposed to her. Her eyes took him in hungrily. His body was a strong and hard feast and she wanted every bite.

"Bend over."

It was a demand, not a request, and Baby Butch folded at the waist, grabbing onto his ankles for support and giving himself to her without hesitation. It was a gift Erika intended to appreciate.

She came behind him, placing her hands on his waist and drawing his ass up and out. She kicked his legs farther apart with the toe of her stiletto, and moved between them. She slid her cock along his ass and cunt teasingly. It was the barest touch, and yet enough to start him moaning and rubbing himself on her stiff dildo, begging for it.

One sudden jackhammer thrust, and Erika was in his cunt to her base. She fucked him without preliminary, without apology, with complete abandon, taking all he gave, devouring his cunt. Her own pussy was consumed with lust, hot and wet, her thighs sticky with desire. She came before he did, deep and hard inside of him, shouting jubilantly.

He stayed on his feet, she gave him credit for that. He was shuddering violently, it was the greatest, perhaps *only*, fuck of his young life, but he was still standing. Even after she came, Erika continued pumping into him, wanting to make him come. She thrust in and out of his soaked cunt, wishing she had a larger cock with her. She wanted him to remember this, wanted him sore and hot for her for days afterward.

"Now. Now, boi." She grew tired of waiting.

Again, he obeyed. God, he was good. He came hard around her cock, swaying on his feet, one hand on the nearest wall for support. If he was crying he didn't appear to notice, gasping for breath and coming again a moment later.

He was spent, heaving beneath her, and still Erika wanted more.

She pulled out of his cunt and slid into his asshole smoothly, so smoothly he only had time to cry out once before she rammed his tight hole. Deciding to be kind, Erika merely stood still with her cock buried in his ass. She would let him do the work this time.

"Jerk yourself off for me, boi," she whispered so low he had to strain to hear her.

He grabbed blindly for his own cock, wrapping one hand around it at its base. He took a deep breath to ground himself, and began stroking his cock, long pulls that sent shivers through them both. With Erika's cock still shoved in his ass, he worked his with mounting need, his movements becoming frantic as wave after cresting wave swept through him. Just as she thought he might break, he began rocking his hips, moving his ass on her cock, fucking himself on it.

Christ, Erika was sure she had never seen anything so damn *hot*. She slid her middle finger onto her own swollen clit and rubbed it until she came again, holding on to his back so she wouldn't topple off of her heels in her urgency.

As if he sensed she needed his strength, Baby Butch paused in his own frantic need and waited for Erika to push herself upright again and pull out of his ass. He straightened up and turned to face her, cock still in his hand. She smiled at what a pretty picture he made—a vision she would take to bed with her that night.

"You can clean yourself up now." She was abruptly all-business again.

She slipped her harness from her waist and stepped daintily out of it, tucking it neatly back into her briefcase. After pulling his jeans back on and tucking his own cock into them, Baby Butch shyly handed her the handkerchief he kept in his back pocket. She smiled gratefully, patting her flushed face. She checked her glossy red lipstick in a compact and smiled again. Flawless.

"Will I...will I see you again?" Baby Butch stammered.

Erika was surprised that she actually felt regretful when she shook her head.

"No, dear. You were sweet, but that's not my style."

Impulsively, she gave him a tender kiss on the check before prancing away, back toward the station. She was now late for a meeting and had a train to catch.

She was utterly aware that his eyes never left her ass as she walked away, and if she swished it just a bit more than was necessary, it was purely for her own amusement.

She did not run into Baby Butch again until Thursday. Oh, how she had relished their encounter again and again in her mind during the days between, although she was reluctant to admit that to herself. A second encounter with the same lover, however sweet that lover may be, however acquiescent, simply did not sit well with her. It was untidy.

Thursday evening, Erika was glancing through an issue of Bazaar during her commute home when she felt someone watching her. She knew before she raised her eyes that it was him. She smiled despite herself at him and his fumbling shyness. She could grow to like that shyness.

He approached her slowly, and fell to one knee in front of her seat. As he handed her a small bunch of obviously hand-picked yellow gerbera daisies, Erika had to laugh. It was all entirely too silly and precious.

At her laughter, Baby Butch's face broke out in a wide grin of delight that Erika found irresistible. She reached for the pretty bouquet.

"All right, honey. Why don't you sit here next to me and tell me your name?"

And once more, she was immediately obeyed.

STRETCH
Kathleen Tudor

"WE'LL BEGIN IN CHILD'S POSE."

I knelt in the center of my yoga mat, my breath coming slow and deep, and at her words, I spread my knees a little bit and hinged forward, arms outstretched along the floor, prostrate. My mind slowly relaxed as I eased into the familiar yoga breath, letting the gentle stretch on my shoulders center me.

"Lift up into tabletop, and begin cat-cow tilts."

Breath still deep and even, I raised myself onto my hands and knees and began to arch and round my back by turns, warming up my spine. My body hummed with a quiet awareness, and I considered taking the liberty of stretching to either side, but resisted, keeping to the required movements with the even flow of my breath.

"On your next exhale, tuck your toes and push up into downward dog."

The pose was like an inverted V, with my hands and feet planted, heels reaching for the mat, and hips lifted to the ceiling. I exhaled a small sigh as I fl owed up into it; in the right frame of mind—on a night like tonight—it could feel like flying.

The warmth of her hand blossomed on my bare back as she placed it carefully between my shoulder blades and pushed, opening my shoulders even more. I sighed at her touch, and felt a tap on my hip reminding me to keep to my breathing. Then her hand eased away, and I held the position. And held it...

I could hold that pose for a long time, but she did not make it easy, making me raise first one leg, then the other, then one arm, then the other, forcing me to use three points to balance. Eventually, the muscles in my arms and shoulders made themselves known. Then they began to ache. Finally, the muscles burned. My breath was harsher, more desperate, and my body quivered with fatigue, sending my breasts dancing.

I folded with a quiet whimper, shifting immediately into child's pose. There was a moment of blissful relief as the muscles in my arms and core went limp with relaxation. Then a sharp crack sounded, and sweet, stinging pain blossomed across my exposed ass. I sucked in a breath, but my arms were still trembling and weak. Another crack. The blow of the riding crop stung my bare skin, and I felt a rush of heat between my legs even as I cried out. I fought the urge to fl inch away or cover myself, searching for my strength—my breath.

Crack.

Crack.

They came at steady intervals, measuring time as she waited for me to overcome my weakness. I whimpered, heart racing as I imagined the disappointed look on her face. Then I planted my hands, straightened my sore arms, and lifted my hips into the air, returning to downward dog. She paced around me twice, waiting for another sign of failure.

"Lift your right leg high, then step it through into a runner's lunge. Crescent pose."

Deep in my lunge, I lifted my hands up off the floor and reached for the ceiling, my upper body straight and my legs taut beneath me. She ran her crop up my right shin, showing approval of the perfect right angle, and I breathed into the stretch. This was another pose I could hold for minutes, but I never knew if this would be the day she chose to push my limits.

"Warrior one," she said after a minute. I dropped my back heel gratefully and considered shortening my stance to make it more comfortable...but no. "Warrior two." A shift of the hips. Arms held out to the sides. Power. "Side angle pose."

Ah, this was a moment of relaxation. I brought my right elbow to my right knee, still deep in the lunge, and leaned over it, bracing myself as my other arm reached straight up past my ear. My breath continued to come in slow, deep, even inhales and exhales, defying the exertion. Belying my arousal.

"Add the arm bind," she said, thoughtfully.

Oh, shit. I leaned even closer to my front leg, my body coming forward, just ahead of my knee, and my right arm went under my leg and around behind my back. My left arm reached behind my back from the other side, and I clasped my hands together, essentially pinning my leg to my torso. It was a surprisingly comfortable pose, and despite the contorted look of it, it wasn't much harder than clasping your hands behind your back as long as you had the hip flexibility to reach around your leg.

But my mistress liked the look of it, and that meant an extended hold.

The sounds of her bare feet as she paced around me were hypnotic, and I focused on the little *slap, slap.* My muscles burned, but I held.... My legs caught fire, but I held.... My body quivered with exhaustion, but I held...

And then my mind began to drift, floating me softly away from the pain and the effort, and taking me somewhere peaceful and soft. Dimly, I was aware of my limbs going limp, and of giving in to gravity, but it wasn't important, was it?

Mistress caught me as I wobbled and slid toward the floor. She pushed and tugged gently at my limbs, and I floated along with her until I found myself face down on the floor once again, my knees tucked to raise my hips high, and this time with my arms behind my back. I felt something tighten around them to keep them there. A yoga strap? It didn't matter. It felt good to be constrained—safe and secure.

I tugged gently against the bonds, feeling them hold my wrists in place, and relaxed fully into my submission. This time, the crop didn't fall right away. Mistress laid the leather fl at against the flesh of my upper back, and I whimpered weakly at the sensation as she trailed it down my spine, between the bare cheeks of my ass, and toward my pussy, which was wet and hot and throbbing. I felt it even through the haze of subspace, like a distant drum, calling...calling...

The sharp smack of the crop on my ass startled me, and I gasped when it connected, though the sting barely penetrated the aroused fog of my mind. Pleasure seemed to roll out from the spot in slow waves, only punctuated by the next hit, and the next.

Mistress took her time, making sure my ass was thoroughly reddened before she bent and untied my wrists. I let my arms slither to the floor bonelessly. She was saying something...it was hard to focus, but the soft croon of her voice was insistent, and I let it pull me toward full awareness again, slowly becoming aware of my stiff muscles and the throb across my ass that now matched the desperate pulsing of my pussy.

"That's a good girl. Come back, now.... Come back..."

"Yes, Mistress," I murmured. She made a sound of approval and reached to pull me to my feet. As I got up, a blanket slid from my back to the floor. When had she put that there?

Then she pressed her lips to mine, and I forgot to wonder.

I nearly collapsed again as my entire body flooded with fire, but her fingers closed tight around my upper arms, and I found the pinch of her nails and the crush of her grip enough to anchor me in place as she ravaged my mouth. She tasted and took, her tongue darting and teasing across my own, her teeth scraping and biting at my lips, and when I moaned, she swallowed that up, too, as if she would devour me.

The ache in my pussy grew to hungry need, and I clenched my hands at my sides even as I squeezed my thighs together, desperate for some release, but smart enough to know better than to take it. When she released me from the kiss, I was breathless with pleasure and desire. My cheeks felt flushed, and my nipples strained to hard peaks.

Mistress caught hold of the crop, which was dangling from the strap on her wrist, and flicked it teasingly across one nipple, and then the other. I gasped and my whole body twitched with arousal at the intermingled pleasure and pain.

"What are you?"

"Yours, Mistress," I said, my answer immediate and sure, even though my mind was still fuzzy. The words, as always, sent the heat of arousal straight to my pussy, already swollen and wet with desire.

She smiled, and I felt a different kind of warmth at having pleased her. "Good girl. And what do I expect out of my things?"

"Perfection, Mistress."

"And that is why we work so hard, isn't it, my love?"

"Yes, Mistress."

"So, we must set aside our urges to play, and finish what we started. Second side."

Second... Oh, Gods above and hells below, she wanted me to finish the yoga lesson. Like this!

"Downward dog." I moved immediately to comply, even as my mind struggled to process that my overwhelming arousal would have to wait. "Tisk, my love, remember your breath! Left leg up, now. Bring it through for a lunge...now up into crescent pose..."

I flowed obediently through the poses as she brought me into the bound arm pose on the second side. The scent of arousal wafted around me with each movement, and I heard the sweet sound of my mistress' deep inhale as she appreciated the delicate aroma. Gods, my hands were so close to my pussy, and yet they might as well have been a mile away!

I yearned to let go of my clasped hands and stretch my fingers to that hot, wet place—to tease and rub and scratch and pinch my way to screaming delight—but I breathed, each deep breath bringing me the scent of my own desire. And I waited.

It wasn't as long, this time—not nearly so long—before she brought her crop to the inside of my right ankle, and started to travel up the straight line of my leg, making slow progress toward my honeyed cunt. Before my eyes, a heavy bead of arousal formed and dripped from my pussy to the mat below. My breath came faster, more desperate, and Mistress tapped her crop against the inside of my thigh as a reminder. Deep. Slow. Oh, mercy!

The little bit of leather continued its journey, and I thought I might die as she let the crop linger on the uppermost part of my inner thigh, tracing tiny circles before my starved eyes as I prayed for it to move higher. Please! Higher!

"You are not breathing correctly," Mistress said. Then she flicked the crop, and I watched in horrified fascination, as the crop twitched back from my leg, and then in, coming down with a *snap* on my wet cunt. I screamed at the shock of the contact, more than the pain. It stung, but not as badly as I'd feared.

I wobbled slightly in my balanced pose, and Mistress stepped forward, bracing my body against hers from behind me. The contact reminded me of why she'd had to punish me in the first place, and I took a deep breath, trying to center myself. Steady...in...out...

The scent of my own arousal was intoxicating. I might have swayed again if Mistress hadn't been there, holding me aloft with her presence against my back and hips. Then she shifted, and the world exploded in sparks of pleasure as her hand slid through the slick folds of my pussy. Mistress hummed her pleasure and approval of my wetness, and I gasped and shuddered under her touch. She pinched her nails into my labia in gentle warning, and I tried desperately to focus on breathing evenly.

Heaven! Hell!

She teased at my slickness, sliding one finger deep inside me as I watched her erotic manipulations from up close. I wanted to cry as I watched her finger slide in and out of me, so close I could almost taste it. Had she known what this pose—this position—would do to me?

She chuckled as she slid her finger in all the way to the knuckle, and I supposed she did know. Breathe. *Breathe.* Her finger slid free of my pussy and she teased gently at the folds of flesh before finally settling directly above my clit. I wanted to hold my breath, or shout, or cry, but instead I inhaled deeply. Mistress made a pleased sound, and her finger descended to tease at the swollen bud. Her other hand curled through the collar at my throat, possessing me, claiming me, and reminding me, all at once.

I managed, somehow, to keep the stutter of pleasure out of my breath, and instead exhaled a soft sigh of pleasure, maybe flavored with a moan. Her finger continued to circle and tease, and I tensed, finally noticing the burn in my legs. How long had I been standing here in this lunge? It ached, and yet the demand of my clit was a much greater ache, and if I stepped out of position, it wouldn't be fulfilled.

Hold. Just...hold. I willed strength into my legs and cried out sharply as Mistress pinched my clit, sending a burst of pleasure through me. My even breaths broke into ragged pants, and my entire body quivered and shook for a new reason as I climbed desperately toward the jagged peak of release. My mistress' breath was just as fast and hard with arousal, and I changed to match her, breathing along with her, sucking in air as I let her lead me over the edge and into oblivion.

I arched back into her when I came, and my knees finally buckled, my arms losing their grip and unfolding as I fell in a mound of pleasure at my mistress' feet. I pulled broken sobs of air into my lungs, feeling the aftereffects of pleasure washing through me as I struggled toward some semblance of poise.

When I finally realized that I was curled into a shuddering ball at my mistress' feet, I pulled myself together with a whimper, rolling onto my belly and pulling my legs back up into child's pose. I waited, arms extended, as she paced around me once again. Then she turned and walked away.

Had I made her angry? Had my failure disappointed her? I bit my lip and breathed deeply through my nose, trying to calm the rising panic at the thought of having let my beloved mistress down.

But when she returned, it was to place a pillow directly behind me and to kneel on it. I felt something hard and cool probe my still-swollen cunt, and I gasped as she lifted my hips and thrust into me, driving her strap-on home.

"You're so gorgeous," she said, rocking against me, driving her cock deep. "Such a good, beautiful girl. You did wonderfully." She moaned as she thrust into me again, and I whimpered as I imagined the way the teasing inner edge of the strap-on was pleasuring her while she fucked me.

"Thank you, Mistress."

"Do you feel strong, my love?" She thrust into me again, quicker now, driving her toy deep inside me. My pussy clenched around the girth of the cock, milking pleasure out of each thrust.

"Yes, Mistress!" She had taught me yoga, and used it as a tool to keep me lean and strong. And sometimes, for more.

My body was still sensitive from her earlier attentions. I received her eagerly, and each moan and sigh I heard from her was transformed alchemically into more and more pleasure for me. My fingertips dug into the mat, and I cried out each time she thrust home, my pussy clenching rhythmically until the rising tide of orgasm carried me away again.

Mistress continued to fuck me, pounding hard until I flowed down from the heights I'd achieved. I cried out with the loss, anyway, when I felt her pull away from me, swearing softly. "Come clean up your mess," she demanded, her voice strained.

I turned, kneeling on the pillow she had just vacated, and she thrust her shining cock toward my face, still slick with my juices.

It had shocked me, the first time she'd done this, to find that I actually enjoyed the slick, rubbery slide of her cock in my mouth. I had expected to detest it—to feel humiliated—but instead, I had loved the pleased whimpers from my mistress' throat, and the way that she had dominated me by forcing my flesh with this toy.

I sucked it into my mouth eagerly, making sure to push back against it as much as I could while I sucked and licked, shoving it against her clit and teasing her to the best of my ability. It was like a game between us, to see if I could make her come just from sucking her fake cock alone.

She bit her lip and groaned, trying to hold off—to make me work for it—but I only grew more frenzied as I sensed how close she was getting. My body flushed with arousal and desire, making me warm all over despite my nakedness, and I sucked harder, my hands resting tensely on my thighs as I'd been trained.

Her hands, unrestricted, tangled in my hair and brushed over my face, rewarding my diligent attention with the sweetness of her love for me. I closed my eyes and focused on the feel of her cock in my mouth, the taste rubbery now that the tang of my arousal was gone, and the way that the pressure of my lips and tongue could make her gasp or moan or clench her fingers in my hair. I felt her draw a nail down my cheek, and breathed deeply, smelling her arousal as it rose around us like a cloud of perfume.

Her breath broke as she grew close, and my body trembled in response. She was so close now.... Just another nudge—just one more sweep of my tongue along the underside of her cock—and I would have her.

Mistress cried out as we both won our little game, and her legs shook with the force of her orgasm. I eased back from her cock, waiting for her to recover, breathless with pleasure at having pleased her.

I was still kneeling, eyes submissively lowered, hands glued to my thighs, when Mistress calmed herself, slipped out of her toy harness, and placed both hands on my head like a blessing. I smiled, warmed from the inside by her affection. "Would you like me to return to my yoga lesson?" I asked.

Mistress laughed. "I think we can find another way to work ourselves out today, don't you?"

SILVIA
THE THIRD OF FOUR ELEMENTAL STORIES
River Light

SILVIA HAD A LIGHT TOUCH, USEFUL FOR THE MAKING OF THE DELICATE jewelry she crafted. She was tall and willowy with eyes so light blue they were almost white. Her white hair fell to her waist and was kept back with a simple but elegant broach at the nape of her neck. Her elfin face and long slender fingers caused many to ask if she played an instrument. She looked like she should play the harp or violin, or at very least, the piano—but the only music she made was in her jewelry.

Her jewelry was exquisite and, unlike many artists, she made her living, a very good one, with her work. She worked with silver, glass, crystal and diamond. Her only deviation was the occasional ruby, a drop of blood on snow and ice. She did not take commissions; each piece she created was born from her mind alone.

Silvia was unmarried and unattached. It seemed her art was her love. There were many who would have liked to call her friend, but if being a friend included the sharing of confidences, there were none who could. She was not haughty, aloof, or cold. It was more that her attention seemed to encircle the room, never just a single person in it.

If she had lovers they did not speak of it, and those who courted her found their advances gently deflected. For all that, she never had a lack of suitors or company, for sitting near to her was to be encircled in a stillness and calm which was as cleansing as bathing in a mountain stream or sacred pool.

Cat found Sylvia irresistible. She was shadow to Silvia's light. Olive skin, dark brown hair kept short by regular trips to her barber, and almost black eyes. She was earth to Silvia's air. Stocky, solid. Cat's fascination with Silvia slowly grew to full-fledged infatuation. She became obsessed with finding a way to connect with her, acutely

165

aware that every advance was deftly turned aside, mystified at Silvia's uncanny ability to never be caught in a commitment of any sort.

Silvia could often be found at play parties, dinner parties or private dungeons. She radiated strength and confidence without being in the least bit showy. She always came alone, watched and left alone. Her looks, her grace in all meanings of the word, and her presence was so striking, however, that she was always invited back—though she never dressed the part nor partook in the activities.

Cat woke up one cold spring morning to the realization that she had decided overnight to place herself in service to Silvia, regardless of Silvia's interest (or lack thereof). She chose the first of May, Beltane, to begin this service. She did not know if Silvia celebrated Mayday, but she felt it appropriate, the symbolism reflecting her own re-birth. They were both attending the annual Leather Fair fundraiser—Silvia to sell her jewelry, Cat volunteering on security. As Silvia set up her wares, Cat wiped her suddenly sweaty palms on her jeans, and without asking re-filled Silvia's cup of water that was sitting on the corner of the booth. Silvia drank, but did not acknowledge the action. For the rest of the day Cat made sure that her cup was always filled.

And so for almost a year she was attentive to Silvia, filling her drink or plate when it became empty, noting her favorite foods and making sure they were at her side when she sat. Opening doors for her, taking her coat when she arrived anywhere, presenting it to her before she needed to ask for it as she left. She knew it was a fine line she walked, and worked very hard not to cross it. She did not hover, did not engage Silvia in conversation any more than others of her acquaintance, nor scamper or fall over herself. Cat had been in service to a number of Tops, and had had her share of bois and girrls in her own service, so had enough experience to pull this off well, if not perfectly.

Her friends noticed of course, and teased her about it, ribbing her for the hopelessness of her devotion, but never in front of the object of her desire. On Silvia's part she was gracious, but never acknowledged that Cat did any more or less for her than anyone else, and never gave any indication that Cat's actions were desirable, or undesirable, in any way.

Then, Silvia broke a pattern that Cat had never seen change. Instead of leaving the party as soon as the evening began to wind to a close, she stayed. She stayed until everyone had left and she, Cat and her hosts were the only ones left. And then she turned slowly and looked at Cat. Looked her in the eye. With a shock Cat understood that Silvia was very much aware of her, of her actions of the past year, and felt ridiculous for ever doubting it.

"Walk with me." Her voice was like dry leaves on a cold fall day. Soft, but crisp and clear. It seemed then that Silvia had never actually spoken to her before this, had never looked at her before this.

As they walked down the front steps Silvia said quietly, "You are very persistent".

Cat couldn't speak, had nothing to say, could not even nod. As they reached the sidewalk she realized that she did not know what kind of car Silvia drove, or even if she drove a car at all.

Silvia put out her hand, palm up. "Your keys."

Cat fumbled in her pocket and dropped them into her palm. Her motorcycle was parked directly in front of the house, a perfectly maintained 1985 Honda 1100 Shadow. Silvia slipped the helmet off the handlebars and passed it to Cat.

"Ahh, I don't have my second helmet." Cat felt like an idiot, but somewhat relieved as she never let anyone drive her bike, and was not sure why she had just passed over the keys.

Silvia ignored her, flipped her leg over the bike and pulled it upright with ease. She started the engine and waited, not looking at Cat. Finally Cat fasted the helmet and slipped onto the unfamiliar back seat.

"Hold on."

As soon as she had her feet on the pegs and her hand on Silvia's waist the bike peeled away from the curb. She drove much, much too fast and yet each move was so skilled and smooth that it was like Silvia's body had grown into the bike and they had become a single unit.

She had always presumed Silvia lived in the apartment above her studio, but they didn't head in that direction. Instead, she turned the bike to the east and headed out of town.

As they merged onto the highway she pushed the throttle all the way forward. It was late and the road was almost empty. Cat watched in shock as the speedometer crept up until it could go no further, but still Cat could swear they continued to pick up speed. She had no idea the bike could actually move that fast. She could feel the adrenalin, but at the same time it was so surreal that a part of her brain was simply not accepting what she was seeing. Silvia wove between the cars like she was on a high speed chase in some cop movie. Her body was upright and completely relaxed. Her hair, caught by the wind and whipped around Cat's face, streamed out behind the both of them, her hair broach gone.

In a very short time they pulled off the highway onto a smaller road, and then an even smaller one, and finally what Cat realized was a long driveway that wove through the forest up the side of the mountain until it finally opened up and ended at a small plateau. To her right the mountain dropped away and Cat had a clear view of the city lights below. The almost full moon cast enough light to illuminate a winding stairway on her left cut into the rock face.

Cat did not know why Silvia reached out her hand as she stepped off the bike until her feet touched the ground and her knees gave out. The hand was strong and steady on her elbow, supporting her until she found her own legs. When she could again stand without assistance, Silvia turned toward the bluff s above her and started up. There was no hand rail, and the rough hewn steps were covered in moss and whatever grass had caught hold in the cracks.

It was strikingly beautiful in its wildness, and Cat felt as though she had stepped back in time, or been transported to the old world.

By the time they reached the top Cat was winded, and tense from watching her footing in the near darkness. After catching her breath she looked up. The house in front of her looked to be built from the same rock they had just climbed, and would have blended into the stone behind if it were not for the fact that the entire front face was window overlooking the mountains, water and city below.

Inside Silvia led her to a large living room and motioned her to sit down on the straight backed chair placed at its center. She felt Silvia's gaze on her again but could not bring herself to look up. She instead stared at the patters of moonlight shining on the floor in front of her, which offered more illumination then the lights turned low in the room, until she heard Silvia walk over to the window where she stood for a time looking out. She turned and stood silhouetted against the moonlight, her face in shadow. A part of Cat's brain noted that her hair was still loose from its clip, that it fell over her shoulders and down her back as though it had been freshly brushed. Where were the tangles from their wild ride? Then Silvia shifted a little and Cat could see her face.

"What is it that you want from me?"

The question was so unexpected that Cat could only gawk, pinned by her gaze and the improbability of it. How could she answer that? How could she put it into words? What did she want? She wanted Sylvia to touch her. She wanted to be given permission to kiss her feet. She wanted to serve her, to do anything to make her happy. She wanted Silvia to hurt her. She wanted everything and anything. Finally Cat did the only thing she felt like she knew to do. She slipped off the chair, approached Silvia's form and dropped to her knees, eyes down. She kept her back straight and her body still.

Silvia let out a long breath, the sigh of the wind through oak trees; an exhalation of breath held in expectation. Cat heard the blood rushing in her ears, felt her heart pound in her chest. Silvia was so still that without being able to see her Cat could have been the only one in the room.

She felt something brush the top of her head—a breeze or a hand? Silvia put her fingers under her chin and tilted her head up. "Do you give yourself to me freely?"

Cat managed to force enough air from her lungs to whisper "yes."

"Without knowing what that may mean?"

"Yes."

The large bay windows behind Sylvia banged open as a sudden guest of wind hit them. Cat jumped. The wind blew around them, shifting and lifting Silvia's hair so that in the moonlight it looked like a cloud around her face. The windows had opened outward, and the lights had gone out at some point, but Cat could not fathom how or why. Her brain felt fuzzy. The wind gusted around the room with an uncanny strength and Cat could feel the air moving around her as if alive. Then the room shifted and she and Silvia lifted off the ground. It was at that point Cat's brain decided to stop processing impossibilities, and she fainted.

CB&O

THE AIR ON HER BARE SKIN WAS COOL, BUT NOT SUCH THAT SHE WAS COLD. A breeze caressed her belly and her thighs, and then something brushed her lips. She shuddered and opened her eyes but could see nothing in the complete darkness. She tried to sit up and only then realized that her naked body was fastened to the floor at hips, shoulders, wrists and ankles. She felt her breasts being caressed but had no sense at all that she was anything but alone. And the caresses did not feel like hands, but instead firmer gusts of the wind that had brushed her as she had awoken. The touch was becoming more firm; on her breasts and face she felt the persistent caresses. Her nipples became hard, not from cold but the intense sensation, and it sent waves of pleasure between her legs. She could feel her thighs brushed, and her lips being parted, her cunt penetrated, stretched wide and filled. She gasped with the intensity of it, the unexpectedness of it. There was no one there, of this she was now sure. It would have had to have been more than one person for her to be stroked on so many parts of her body at once, and the silence was too complete. All she heard was her own quickening breathing and gasps. She felt something pushing into her ass and opening her wide, filling her. Her body began to tremble violently with the intensity of being so completely filled and caressed. She cried out and strained against her bonds, not to get away, but to reach toward her tormentor. With her gasped inhalation, the presence filled her mouth, her nostrils, slipping down her throat, filling her lungs: like a deep kiss, like fingers exploring her, like a cock down her throat. She could not breathe, and yet, needed no breath. She felt suspended, skewered as though on a spit from mouth through to cunt, the movement in and around her so intense that she felt on the verge of being torn apart, every bit of her body, inside and out, was being stroked and filled. When the first waves of pleasure crashed into her, she screamed, her body bucking and writhing as she came again and again. But there was no release, no relenting when her shudders finally subsided. She was still surrounded and filled, and even as she felt spent, she felt her body respond to the persistent caress, the intimate invasion; felt the pleasure building in her again.

When the touch finally stopped, she was beyond exhaustion. Just before the deeper darkness of sleep claimed her she caught a glimpse of what could have been Silvia's white hair—or could have been phantom light behind her eyelids.

The next time she awoke, the darkness and her bonds were gone. She sat up slowly. The room looked to be half-cavern, half-windowless grand hall. Every inch of wall was carved. In some places it was a random pattern, in others people, animals or plants where represented. Far above her, the rounded roof seemed to have an entire story etched into its face. There was a defused light that seemed to come from everywhere and nowhere, and she could see neither windows, nor a door. She saw shadowy recesses in the walls, and nothing else, other than the large pile of animal furs in which she sat. The floor was bare stone. A large platter heaped with food was beside her on the floor, with a mug and a pitcher of cool clear water next to it. She eat and drank, circled the cavern, slept, eat again. She found a hole in the stone floor at the back of one of the recesses that seemed the only thing that could possibly be used as a lavatory, and so she did, not hearing her urine reach the bottom. Her clothes were gone, but she was not chilled, and the furs were comfortable and warm.

She slept again, and it was the unexpected sound of footsteps that awoke her this time. Without thought she scrambled out of the bedding and knelt, head down, arms clasped behind her back, spine straight. The footsteps stopped in front of her.

"Cat." Her voice was wind through the grasses. She had never spoken her name before, and Cat trembled from the pleasure of hearing it, the thought of being held in Silvia's mouth and then released.

Cat raised her head and was caught by her gaze. Silvia wore what she always wore, and yet Cat realized she had never seen her clothes before, had never, in all the years she had known her, noted them. She wore white silk shot through with ice blue. Neither dress, nor robe, nor rags, it fell, or more accurately moved, about her in soft folds and hard edges. Overwhelmed by the intensity of Silvia's gaze Cat dropped her eyes again, only to feel Silvia's hand around her throat, bushing her back onto the furs. Her warm lips and persistent hands were decidedly human. This time it was slower; lips, tongue and fingers coaxing the pleasure from her body, sharp teeth and nails eliciting cries of pleasure and pain, and when she came Silvia let her cling to her for long moments.

 catso

SILVIA WAS SOFT AND GENTLE, THE WARM BREEZE ON A LAZY SUMMER afternoon. She was playful as the sea wind slapping the sails on schooners and fishing boats; she was as still as the eye of the hurricane or the moment before a storm; she was the cutting arctic wind in the middle of an ice storm. She was stillness and wild, her strength could smash buildings or gently lift a feather from the ground. She was unpredictable: wild, both as a tiger is wild and a wren is wild.

She never appeared to her again, as though after reassuring Cat that she was in Silvia's hands and no other's, she had no need. But each night Cat was visited in the blackness. Her body caressed or tortured following no pattern that Cat could discern. She lived for those nights, for the screams of pleasure or pain being ripped from her body and tossed around the cavern. She lived for them, and was terrified of them. At the softest whisper she would begin to tremble, from anticipation and from fear. Terrified that this time, if Silvia should choose pain, it would be the night that Cat could no longer bear it. And there were nights that she couldn't—but with no way to change her mind that became meaningless. Meaningless except for the long day of waiting where she would play every pain or pleasure over in her mind, reliving each exquisite touch. Drowning in the memories of her body being used so completely by another. Her body was never marked, and though many times she thought she would, she never lost consciousness.

Each night her mistress grew more skilled at bringing her to the edge of madness or unconsciousness without pushing her over. She knew instinctively to spread and open herself at the first hint of a caress. She did not understand how it was that she served her mistress, what purpose she served, but she accepted that Silvia would take what she wanted; that it was not her place to question.

രജ്ഞ

SHE NEVER FOUND HERSELF BOUND AGAIN, BUT SOMETIMES SHE WOULD awaken to the feel and sound of the howling wind, and it was simply the strength of that wind against her chest and limbs which would hold her motionless against the floor.

She had no sense of time—of days, weeks or months. No idea how long she had been living this dream. She stopped thinking about the past or the future—the cavern, the present, her mistress became her world. Then, one day while she stood reading the pictures carved into the walls, running her fingers over them and thinking of Silvia carving them, she suddenly sensed someone else in the room with her. She spun around and was shocked to see her mistress standing behind her. Her breath caught in her throat; she tried to drop to her knees but she was captured and held in her gaze, frozen.

Silvia's eyes were not human. The edges of her seemed to fade and sharpen as though she might blow away, but there was no softness anywhere in her. Half-apparition, half-flesh, she stood before Cat—terrible and beautiful. Cat was shaking with fear by the time Silvia took her, brought her down to the cold floor of the cavern and savaged her. Her mistress did not seem to see her or to know her and Cat fought back, panic engulfing her. She struggled under Silvia, hearing her own screams of pain as though ripped from another's throat. She could taste blood in her mouth and she could feel her body respond to her mistress even in her cruelty or madness, the pleasure and pain mixed in a whirlwind too intense to bear.

CORED

SHE AWOKE IN HER OWN BED. IT TOOK LONG MINUTES BEFORE SHE COULD place herself. Before the alienness of her own home shifted into the familiar. She lay still, trying to sort through the waves of conflicting emotions, watched the minute hand on her clock slowly move from the one to the twenty. Finally she sat up. Her muscles screamed. She looked down. Scratches, cuts and bruises covered her body and every movement reminded her that she had more muscles than she could count.

Out of habit she opened the front door and was not surprised to see her newspaper on the doorstep, like always. She picked it up and looked for the date. Just over two years. She stared at the numbers for a long time—willing them to make sense.

All had been taken care of. She had been in South America looking for stones for Silvia, had taken a leave at work, was paid well enough to keep her apartment, was back when expected, and just in time for her welcome home party. Her phone, newspaper delivery, and internet had all been re-activated the day before she arrived back, and a friend had filled her fridge. Her work called to confirm that it would be fine for her to start back on Tuesday, instead of Monday. Already it was just memory. Already it was starting to feel like a dream as the daily routine moved in to take its place.

She did not bottom again and did not miss it. She became stone, but did not miss it. Her body had been swept clean, had been used to its fullest—or filled completely—so she could not miss it.

Every now and then their eyes would meet and Silvia would hold her gaze just a fraction longer than necessary; and so she never doubted the reality of what had happened, no matter how dreamlike it became. When a pretty femme whom Cat had been eyeing suddenly left on an errand overseas for Silvia, she only smiled knowingly.

Then, one day, before the whispers of her agelessness grew too loud, Silvia closed up shop and left.

Cat never saw her again

Each Beltane she would go alone to the cliff s overlooking the ocean and stand, eyes closed, feel the wind buffet her face and remember. Sometimes she would wake up abruptly in the middle of the night, and for a moment in the darkness she would forget and spread her legs. Then, one morning, Cat looked in the mirror and saw a stranger with her eyes looking back at her. She ran her fingers over her wrinkled face and through her white hair. Soon after, Cat made up her last will. In it, she requested that her ashes be thrown to the wind from the top of the cliffs, on May Day.

THE AUTHORS

KATHLEEN DELANEY-ADAMS is a stone high femme porn author and spoken word performer. Kathleen is the artistic director of *BODY HEAT: Femme Porn Tour*, now in its seventh year. Look for her work in several upcoming anthologies including *Best Bondage Erotica 2014* and *Kinky Couples Erotica*.

VALERIE ALEXANDER is a freelance writer who lives in Arizona. Her work has been previously published in *Best of Best Women's Erotica*, *Best Lesbian Erotica*, *The Harder She Comes*, *Best Bondage Erotica* and other anthologies. Please visit her at **valeriealexander.org**.

EVEY BRETT (eveybrett.wordpress.com) lives in Arizona with the Lipizzan mare that inspired her books *Capriole, Levade* and *Passage*. She has numerous erotic books and stories with publishers including Loose Id, Carina Press and Cleis Press and was a Fellow at the Lambda Literary Retreat for Emerging LGBT Authors.

RACHEL KRAMER BUSSEL (rachelkramerbussel.com) is the editor of *Cheeky Spanking Stories; Bottoms Up; Spanked; Best Bondage Erotica 2013; Twice the Pleasure: Bisexual Women's Erotica; Orgasmic; Fast Girls; Women in Lust; Going Down; Suite Encounters: Hotel Sex Stories; The Big Book of Orgasms; Baby Got Back: Anal Erotica* and many others.

SACCHI GREEN has published stories in a hip-high stack of erotic books, and edited eight anthologies, including *Lesbian Cowboys* (winner of a Lambda Literary Award) and *Wild Girls, Wild Nights*. Her collection, *A Ride to Remember*, is published by Lethe Press. Find her at **sacchi-green.blogspot.com** or on Facebook.

KATYA HARRIS lives in the UK with her boyfriend, daughter and three crazy rat boys. You can find her on Twitter @Katya_Harris and on Facebook. She hopes that you like what she's written and that you'll come back for more.

Besides writing erotic fiction, **JESSICA LENNOX** enjoys discussing human behavior and gender theory, traveling, and reading books! Her erotic work can be found in *Anything Goes: Queer Lesbian Erotica; Curvy Girls; Girl Fever; Spank!; Where the Girls Are; Hurts So Good; Rubber Sex; Best Women's Erotica 2008*, and other erotic anthologies.

ANNABETH LEONG's lesbian erotica has appeared in many anthologies, including *Lesbian Cops* and *Baby Got Back, Ladies Who Love*, and *Like Hearts Enchanted*. Her kinky erotica has appeared in *Spankalicious, Best Bondage Erotica 2013*, and more. She blogs at annabethleong.blogspot.com.

RIVER LIGHT (RiverDark.ca) is a writer and sex educator from Vancouver, Canada. When not tending to her family she is writing and reading porn, teaching kink workshops and creating a scene. Find her erotica in a variety of anthologies. She is working on a book of essays and stories.

LULA LISBON is a queer-identified femme, passionate about history, dark music, and craft beers. She loves to knit and design, and pole dances to stay fit. Along with two very opinionated kitties, Lula resides in Philadelphia, PA—the setting for many of her stories.

EVAN MORA's stories of love, lust and other demons have appeared in various editions of *Best Lesbian Romance* and *Best Lesbian Erotica*, as well as *Where the Girls Are, Girl Fever*, and *The Harder She Comes*, among others. She lives in Toronto.

GISELLE RENARDE is a queer Canadian, avid volunteer, contributor to more than 100 anthologies, and award-winning author of books like *Anonymous, The Red Satin Collection*, and *My Mistress' Thighs*. Ms Renarde lives across from a park with two bilingual cats that sleep on her head.

JEAN ROBERTA (jeanroberta.com) teaches in a Canadian university. Approximately 100 of her erotic stories appear in anthologies, including four *Dr. Athena Chalkdust* stories. Her historical novella, *The Flight of the Black Swan*, and her collection of historical lesbian erotica, *The Princess and the Outlaw and Other Stories* are available at lethepressbooks.com.

TERESA NOELLE ROBERTS writes sexy stories for lusty romantics of all persuasions. Her work has appeared in *Best Bondage Erotica 2014*; *The Big Book of Bondage*; *The Harder She Comes: Butch-Femme Erotica*; and other provocatively titled anthologies. Look for BDSM romances and the paranormal *Duals and Donovans* series from Samhain.

STYX ST. JOHN currently lives in Anchorage, Alaska. After twenty-something years of working retail, getting a bachelor's in English and dealing with the weather, she decided to try and reach for her dream of becoming a published writer. This is her first story.

KAREN TAYLOR first started writing erotic short stories to seduce and intrigue author Laura Antoniou. It worked; they've been married for fifteen years. Find her stories in *The Academy*, book 4 in *Antoniou's Marketplace* series, *The Love That Never Dies* and *Bondage by the Bay*, among other fine titles.

MARY TINTAGEL is a new British writer who lives on the fringes of Sherwood Forest. Mary enjoys archery, rock climbing, spelunking and walking her dogs. She has never jumped out of a moving airplane unless it was absolutely necessary.

KATHLEEN TUDOR's (KathleenTudor.com) work appears in *Boss: To Serve and Be Served*, *Take Me*, *My Boyfriend's Boyfriends*, *Anything for You*, *Best Bondage Erotica 2012*, *Hot Under the Collar*, and many more. She is co-editor of *Like Hearts Enchanted*. Watch for more in 2014. Contact her at **PolyKathleen@gmail.com**.

BETH WYLDE (bethwylde.com) writes what she likes to read, which is a little bit of everything. Her muse is an equal opportunity smut bunny that believes everyone, no matter their kink, color, gender or orientation is entitled to love, acceptance and hot sex! Email her at **b.wylde@yahoo.com**.

THE MISTRESS

D.L. KING would like to lie around, doing nothing, but instead, she spends far too much time in front of the computer. *She Who Must Be Obeyed: Femme Dominant Lesbian Erotica* is her eleventh anthology. She is also the editor of *Slave Girls: Erotic Stories of Submission, Under Her Thumb: Erotic Stories of Female Domination, Seductress: Erotic Tales of Immortal Desire, The Harder She Comes: Butch/Femme Erotica* (winner of the Lambda Literary Award and Independent Publisher Book Awards gold medalist), *Spankalicious: Erotic Adventures in Spanking, Voyeur Eyes Only: Vegas Windows, Carnal Machines: Steampunk Erotica* (Independent Publisher Book Awards gold medalist), *Spank!, The Sweetest Kiss: Ravishing Vampire Erotica* and *Where the Girls Are: Urban Lesbian Erotica* (Lambda Literary Award finalist). The author of dozens of short stories, her work can be found in various editions of *Best Lesbian Erotica, Best Women's Erotica, The Mammoth Book of Best New Erotica*, as well as such titles as *Girls Who Score, Girl Fever, Fast Girls, Girl Crazy, Luscious, Broadly Bound, Gotta Have It, Sex in the City: New York* and *Please Ma'am*, among others. She has authored a collection of fem dom stories, *Her Wish is Your Command*, as well as two novels of female domination and male submission, *The Melinoe Project* and *The Art of Melinoe*. She also publishes and edits the erotica review site, *Erotica Revealed*. Find out more at **dlkingeortica.com** and **dlkingerotica. blogspot.com**.